Aziza had wan

How could she deny

written on her face, stamped into her eyes? But did she still want it?

Fool that she was, the answer was yes.

And, double fool that she was, he must have seen that truth in her eyes. He pulled her toward him with a strength she could not resist, and the next moment his mouth came down hard on hers, brutal, ruthless, demanding, but in the same moment shockingly sensual. White heat flew through her veins, leaving her stunned that she actually didn't go up in flames with the primitive nature of her unexpectedly wild response. Her legs seemed to melt in the heat, her head spinning in stunned delirium. With no control over her actions, she opened her lips to his, let him plunder the soft interior of her mouth, met the invasion of his tongue with the dance of her own.

Kate Walker was born in Nottingham, UK, but grew up in West Yorkshire. She met her husband at university in Wales and originally worked as a children's librarian. After the birth of her son she returned to her old childhood love of writing. Her first book was published in 1984. She now lives in Lincolnshire with her husband (also a writer), and two cats who think they rule her life.

Books by Kate Walker

Harlequin Presents

Olivero's Outrageous Proposal
A Question of Honor

Royal & Ruthless

A Throne for the Taking

Return of the Rebels

The Devil and Miss Jones

The Powerful and the Pure

The Return of the Stranger

Italian Temptation!

The Proud Wife

The Greek Tycoons

The Greek Tycoon's Unwilling Wife
The Good Greek Wife?

Visit the Author Profile page
at Harlequin.com for more titles.

Kate Walker

Destined for the Desert King

H HARLEQUIN PRESENTS®

ISBN-13: 978-0-373-13397-0

Destined for the Desert King

First North American Publication 2015

Copyright © 2015 by Kate Walker

The publisher acknowledges the copyright holder
of the additional work:

Christmas at The Chatsfield
Copyright © 2015 by Harlequin Books S.A.

Special thanks and acknowledgment are given to Maisey Yates
for her contribution to The Chatsfield series.

Recycling programs
for this product may
not exist in your area.

Printed in U.S.A.

Destined for the Desert King

This book has to be dedicated to my editor Pippa,
who asked for Nabil's story
and so sparked off the idea for it.

And to my students—
the wonderful Walkers' Stalkers—whose
friendship and interest at our writing retreats
more than encouraged me to finish it.

CHAPTER ONE

'Happy anniversary!'

Nabil bin Rashid Al Sharifa, Sheikh of Rhastaan, raised the glass in his hand high in a gesture of congratulation and angled it in the direction of the two honoured guests at the party. The couple who were celebrating today and who, in spite of everything in the past, were now his two greatest friends.

'Congratulations on ten years together. Ten happy years.'

It was the last three words that caught in his throat and almost closed it off, choking them back from his tongue. Ten happy years they had been for his friends, but if he was given the chance there was no way he would want to live through the past decade over again.

'To Clemmie and Karim,' he tried again.

The elegant dark-haired woman, regal as the Queen she truly was in the scarlet robe, heavily embroidered in gold, turned a warm, generous smile in his direction while at her side, Sheikh Karim al Khalifa, like Nabil more sombrely but equally magnificently attired in the flowing robes and headdress of his country, lifted his own glass in acknowledgement of Nabil's toast. It was a moment that no one could ever have anticipated happening ten years before, when Clemmie had been destined to be Nabil's arranged wife, but his headstrong passion for the younger Sharmila had led him to reject her and marry his new, pregnant lover. No one then would have predicted that this huge party would be organised in the Rhastaanian palace to celebrate their ten years of love and marriage...

Of children.

Abruptly Nabil put his glass down on the nearest table, the fine crystal clattering harshly against the polished surface. Even if he hadn't already been told the happy news, it was impossible not to notice the slight swell of Clemmie's belly under the burnished red silk of the floor-length gown. Clementina had always been beautiful. Even when he had been in the throes of the foolishly righteous—or so he had believed—anger and mutiny that had driven him to reject her, he'd had to acknowledge that. But now, with her curvaceous form enriched by her early pregnancy, she had a glow about her that was positively incandescent.

'Congratulations,' Nabil repeated once more, forcing himself to smile at his friends.

He wanted to smile to show that he was happy for them. He *was* happy for them, deep down in his heart. But at the same time he couldn't help contrasting the richness of their life when compared with his own.

What they had in abundance, and what he needed so badly now, but he didn't see a way of discovering the same happiness for himself.

Ten years ago, when they had been starting out on their journey into married happiness, he had thought he had it all. A beautiful wife at his side, a child growing inside her, the future of his country secured against the swirling darkness of uprising that had threatened. Young fool that he'd been—young, blind, heedless, headstrong fool!—he'd thought only of his longing to rebel against the hand that fate had dealt him.

So he'd rebelled all right, and by doing so he'd tied himself into that fate even tighter. He'd locked himself in and thrown away the key.

'Ten wonderful years!'

Karim's voice might have been lifted, projected to reach the whole room and the audience of his guests and peers who thronged the huge space, but his eyes were only on his wife. They were in their own private world and unconsciously Clemmie's hand reached up to rest gently on the barely visible swell, the promise of their unborn child in her belly.

The moment seemed to hang on the air, thick with emotion and a touch of secret sensuality, until it was broken by a flurry of sound and a whirl of movement as two small bodies careered across the room and flung themselves at their parents with shrieks of delight.

'Adnan, Sahra…' Clemmie's voice was soft and warm even as she tried to make her words into the gentlest of reproofs. 'Is that any way for a prince and princess to behave at such a public event?'

'But it's Mummy and Daddy's party,' Adnan declared with all the confidence of his just five years of age. 'Not a pub-publicked 'vent!'

Another smile passed between Clemmie and Karim at their son's declaration, and the boy's father let his hand drop to ruffle the mop of shining black hair with easy affection. It was the sort of warmth that Nabil had never known with his own father, a coldly distant man who barely knew his son's name.

'It's both,' Karim said quietly and something in that tone made Nabil move sharply and abruptly, half-turning towards the door and then forcing himself back again. As host for this event, it was his place to stay where he was, to ensure that the celebrations went perfectly, but right now...

Go on...

The words weren't actually spoken but he could almost hear them on the air. It was just a flicker of a response that drew his attention to Clemmie's fine-boned face, but as soon as she had caught his eye, she made the tiniest of gestures with her dark head, indicating the doors out on to the terrace. The complete understanding of what was in his thoughts was there in the warmth of her smile, the flicker of her eyes towards the open doors that spelled escape and freedom from the public ceremony. She had recognised his response, knew the thoughts that were in his head—and was happy to let him take the time to breathe that he needed.

'Now—weren't you going to sing that special song?'

Her question drew everyone's attention to the two children and Clemmie, focusing on her and away from Nabil.

With a silent whisper of thanks to the woman who his father had once decreed should be his bride but instead, with her true husband, had become one of his dearest friends, Nabil took the opportunity that presented itself and moved, silent and soft-footed, across the marble floor and out on to the balcony.

The coolness of a faint breeze stirred the robes he wore, making them swirl softly as he moved, and the blackness of the night was eased by the cold glow of the moon just coming up over the horizon. Roughly Nabil dragged in long, much-needed breaths of air as he paced down the long stone-flagged gallery before coming to a halt and, resting his hands on the high parapet, stared out at the lights that burned in the darkness beyond the walls of the palace. To where the people his country had completed their daily business, and now went about the procedure of settling for the night, getting their children ready for bed, kissing them goodnight.

'Damnation!'

His hand formed into a fist, pounding down against the roughness of the stone as he faced the images in his mind. It seemed that today everything around him conspired to drive home to him how much he should have. How much he had once thought he had only to have it all snatched away. In a gesture that was so much of a habit he barely noticed these days, he lifted a hand to rub at the side of his face where a scar marked his cheekbone, not really concealed by the thick black beard he had grown in an attempt to disguise it. Not that it had worked. The white line that scored through his skin was still there like the mark of Cain every time he looked in the mirror; reminding him.

A sudden sound, soft and slow in the darkness, reminded him of just where he was, the open expanse of the palace grounds between him and the walls that surrounded them. Unwanted and unwelcome, the memories came creeping back, pushing him to take a single step backwards, away from the edge, into the shadows. Tonight it seemed that the darkness hid potential for danger, for destruction.

Or was that just his own state of mind?

At his left hand side, the sound came again, soft and light, bringing his head round so fast it made his thoughts spin. Who?

'Highness.'

The voice was low, quiet, but with an edge of apprehension marking it as he glared into the darkness. It was also obviously female, something that should have made his tension ease, relaxing his shoulders. But there was something about the sound of her voice that tugged at memories he had thought long buried, dragging them to the surface of his mind when he had no wish to revisit them. Memories that had taught him that no one, man or woman, was truly to be trusted.

'Who's there? Show yourself.'

A rustle of fabric sweeping the stone flags, the whisper of soft shoes on the hard ground and she stepped forward, into the moonlight. Small and slender, pale face, dark hair, an embroidered wrap swathing her body and up and over her head, covering her almost completely.

For a second it seemed that his heart juddered in his chest, his breath catching, so that the attempt at words escaped him almost without thought.

'Sharmila?'

He didn't believe in ghosts—and yet something spoke to him...

'Your pardon, Sheikh.'

Her hands, steepled together, came out to touch her forehead as she lowered her head in a salute of respect and submission. The gesture made him catch two things. First there was the wave of perfume, sandalwood and flowers, rich and sensual. It swirled around him like scented mist, putting his senses on alert, but this time in a new and very different way. He inhaled deeply, felt the aroma work its way through him like some rich wine so that he had to blink hard to clear his vision. That was when he noticed the second thing—that the left hand she had lifted to her forehead had a—not a deformity—a tiny twist to the little finger that made it sit not quite straight against her hand.

From somewhere deep a memory stirred in his mind,

surfaced and was then gone again. Had he seen her before—and if so when?

But the woman—a young woman—was speaking again, her words bringing his attention back to the present.

'Forgive me, Your Highness. I didn't know that anyone else was out here. I thought no one would notice me.'

Aziza's voice trembled in her own ears. She should have known that she could be caught out here, like this, away from the celebrations in the main hall. She also knew that Sheikh Nabil was a hard, demanding man, totally focused on security within his palace. Who could blame him after what had happened? But the noise and the heat of the anniversary party had all been rather too much for her. That and watching her older sister Jamalia flirt outrageously—or as outrageously as she dared in front of their parents—with every eligible young man who was present.

She had had to get away from the party, away from playing second fiddle to Jamalia. Away from her father's constant scrutiny of his second daughter, the one who might as well be a servant because of the way he expected her to keep in the background. She was supposed to stay there and act as chaperone. Of course Jamalia didn't want her there; and to tell the truth Aziza had wanted to be anywhere but with her sister. She hadn't even wanted to come to this party in the first place. But her father had insisted. Everyone who was anyone would be at the celebration, and their absence would most definitely be noticed if they weren't.

'Not mine,' Aziza had muttered under her breath but her mother's glare in her direction had made her think more than twice about saying the words aloud. So she had swallowed down her protest, had dressed herself in the deep pink silk gown that had been provided and had followed in her parents' footsteps into the golden palace for the evening.

Jamalia of course had thought that her reluctance was only because her sister didn't want to act as chaperone. That and the fact that Aziza was always ill at ease with the young men who flocked to her side. But there was more to it than that.

And now the real reason why she had been so unwilling to come tonight was standing right before her, tall and powerful, the scent of his skin swirling round her, his dark head blotting out the light of the moon so that she was totally in his shadow.

It was a place she was used to, she acknowledged privately. She had always been in Nabil's shadow, always trailing after him from the moment when, as a lordly twelve-year-old on a visit to her parents' home, he had flung himself from the saddle of a horse that had seemed skyscraper high to her diminutive five-year-old status and tossed the reins in the direction of a groom.

'Who are you?'

The question, hard and sharp, was exactly the same one that Nabil had demanded of her all those years before so that for the moment she didn't recognise the fact that it had come from Nabil and not from her memories. It was only when she saw his mouth clamp tight together in the darkness of the rich beard he now sported that she realised he had asked her *now* and not then.

'Just a maid.'

She looked the part well enough, she reflected. The pink gown wasn't new, of course, but one handed down from Jamalia. 'It will do for Zia,' her father had said. Because Aziza wasn't the one being paraded in front of the Sheikh in the hope of an advantageous marriage, as her sister was.

'I—I am with Jamalia, sire.'

Instinct made her spread her skirts, sweeping into a low and careful curtsey. She hoped that the obeisance she showed him might ease the tension she could feel coming in waves from the tall, powerful man before her. Her mother had worried that she would stumble into some awkward situation if she went off on her own, and right now it seemed that Naddiya had been right. But the truth was that this situation was not of the politicking and plotting that her parents were obsessed with and much more on a personal level.

'Your name?'

'Zia, sire.'

Some instinct made her give the nickname everyone in her family used. At least that way he might not associate her directly with her parents and their political manoeuvrings. It was impossible to avoid the sting of wry reflection at the thought of just why her given name had been shortened to this form.

'Aziza, hmm?' her father had said. *'A name that means "the beautiful one" for someone so small and plain? I think not. Let's face it, our second daughter could never be the beautiful one when compared with her sister.'* He had shortened her name to Zia and it had stuck.

'I needed some air. I ask your pardon...'

An impatient, dismissive wave of his hand flicked away her explanation, making her break off in confusion. Had he forgiven her for being here—hiding, as he would see it, in the darkness? She'd taken a real risk, knowing how tight the security still was in the place. So she would only have herself to blame if this all turned nasty.

Perhaps she should have given him her own name, but her heart kicked inside at just the thought. All those years ago, from the moment that the twelve-year-old Nabil had turned to notice her—*her*, not her two years older sister Jamalia—she had lost her heart in the blink of an eye. For days after that, she had followed him round like a little puppy, always at his heels, hoping for another glance her way. She was so unused to being singled out for any attention that his tolerance for her, the stunning effect of his smile, even then had knocked her off balance. She had fallen head over heels into a youthful adoration that was all the more potent for having been so innocent and juvenile. She had given him her childish heart and all that had happened since had meant that he still had a hold on her emotions that no one else had ever quite managed to displace him from.

He was so instantly recognisable—apart from the black beard that shaded his angular jaw—she would have known who he was immediately. But there was something deeply personal that held her back from giving him her name. What if he didn't remember her? If he stared at her blankly, unable to recall any Aziza from so long ago? Her father would have laughed at the thought that he might recall her, and it was foolish to let herself be hurt by the possibility—the probability—that he would not remember her as she did him. But something small and hidden deep inside her shrank from even taking the risk.

'If you will forgive me…'

She had turned towards the doors into the main palace when he stirred again and his voice came from behind her.

'Don't go!'

Nabil had no idea what made him say it. Why the hell should he want anyone to stay with him when at last he had found the solitude and silence of the balcony that should have been balm to his barren soul? But, now that this slip of a woman was so obviously intent on hurrying away and leaving him there, he knew a sudden new rush of emptiness piled on emptiness that had always been there, and the words had escaped him without thought.

'Highness?'

She hadn't been expecting them either. It was obvious from the way that she started as if she'd been hit, froze, then whirled back to face him. In the moonlight her eyes were wide and dark.

'Don't go. Stay a while.'

He pitched it as a command, not a request, and saw the change in her expression as he did so. For a second her clouded gaze slid to the open door, where the light from the ballroom spilled out on to the balcony, the hum of voices and clink of glasses drifting out to them on the night air. But then she obviously decided on the wisdom of obeying him and she dipped once more into a deferential curtsey.

'And stop doing that,' Nabil growled. It wasn't subservience or submissiveness he wanted now. What he wanted was…

What?

Damnation, if he couldn't answer that himself then what could he ask from her?

'Sir' was all she said, but there was a new light in her eyes and an unexpected tilt to the pretty chin as she looked up at him. Not defiance, quite, but there was something very different there. Something that tugged on a sliver of memory that flickered for a moment in his thoughts and then went out again.

She kept her distance now, deliberately leaving several paces between them. But it was not enough to prevent the swirl of her perfume reaching out to him. The richness of sandalwood and jasmine tantalised his nostrils, stirring his senses in a way he hadn't experienced in years. The kick of his heart and sudden heating of his blood was a shock to his system, making his pulse pound in unexpected response. It was so long since he had felt this way that the rush of sexual hunger made his senses spin. For years the most beautiful, sensual women had tried to create this effect in him and failed, and now some small, insignificant female had set his libido smouldering in a way he had almost forgotten could happen.

'Should I fetch you a drink?'

She had seen the way his tongue had slipped out, moistening unexpectedly dry lips, and had misread the gesture. It jolted him to think that she had been watching him so closely.

'No—I'm fine.'

What was she? A maid? 'I'm with Jamalia,' she had said, and she must mean the eldest daughter of the El Afarim family.

He knew a scowl had darkened his face but he made no effort to hold it back. The thought of Farouk El Afarim and his family, the reasons why they were parading the beautiful Jamalia before him, brought with it a scratch of discomfort that scraped over his nerves. He had wanted to forget for tonight—needed no reminders of the unrest that was threatening again, the importance of ensuring El Afarim's loyalty with a valuable treaty to stop him defecting to the rebels' side.

'Just stay—and talk.'

'About what?'

'Anything. For example…' He waved a hand to draw her eyes away from the balcony on which they stood, towards the lights of the city and beyond, to the horizon where the mountains lifted towards the sky. 'What do you see out there?'

'What do I see?' Another questioning glance but she still turned from him, taking several steps towards the parapet, leaning against it as she gazed out at the scene spread below them. 'Why do you ask?'

Another question he couldn't answer. He had to admit that he wanted to see that view—and all it represented—through her eyes. If it was the price of everything that was to come, then he wanted to know he was not the only one who valued it. That it was worth the decision he had made.

'Humour me.'

The truth was that he wanted to keep her with him a while longer. To talk with someone who was not connected with the demands and debates, the treaties and the dissensions that had filled his life these past months. Someone who didn't need to be treated diplomatically all the time, or who made him watch his tongue so carefully that it felt almost bitten through with the times he'd had to hold back impatient words.

To spend more time with someone who stirred his senses in a way that no one had in the time that he could remember. It was like coming alive again and he wanted more of it.

For a moment he seriously considered making a move on her. She was up for it; there was no doubt about that. He could see it in her face, hear it in her voice, in that little breathless hiccup that shaded each word. If he did try to take things further, she would not resist.

He let those seconds linger, tasted them on his tongue, in his blood. He savoured the feelings that had been almost dead to him for so long, welcoming them, relishing them. Then, slowly and reluctantly, he let them go, throwing them aside as no longer for him. If there was one thing that the past ten years had taught him, it was that that sort of empty relationship, the connection that blinded him for a few hours, driving away the darkness for a night, in the end had nothing that was a real result. The darkness was still there when he woke and it always felt so much the worse in the cold light of day after having been hidden behind the intoxication of wild and mindless sex in a heated bed for the night.

He should let her go. He should turn and walk away but his senses held him captive. And when she spoke again just the sound of her voice was like a signal, beckoning him closer.

'What I see…'

Aziza was both glad and reluctant to turn her eyes away from the man before her and focus them on the scene below. It wasn't easy. In the moment that she had turned away he must have moved closer so that she heard the soft whisper of his robes drifting over the stone. She could almost feel the heat of his body touching her, and the scent of musk and clean skin that swirled around her like perfumed smoke made her senses swim. It dried her lips, tightened her throat so that she snatched in a raw breath to ease the feeling.

'You must know what there is there now—even if you can't actually see it. You must look out at it every day and see the sea to the right—Alazar over towards the mountain—and here…'

Her voice cracked, breath shortening as the arm she used to gesture with caught on the fine material of his robe, bringing home to her just how close he was now.

'And here…?'

Was that stiffness in his tone created by anything like the way her own tongue felt as she struggled to speak? Was it possible that he had actually come closer because he too recognised the darkly sensual tug of attraction that she had known from the moment she had looked up into his face, focusing on the dark depths of his eyes, the rich sensuality of his beautifully shaped mouth in the black shadow of his beard? This was nothing of the childish, immature hero-worship of the five-year-old who had first met Nabil and given her heart to him. It wasn't even anything like the ardent crush that hero-worship had developed into as she had discovered the passionate feelings of adolescence.

No, this was the response of a grown woman to a mature and powerful man. A man who roused all that was feminine in her. But a man she must keep her distance from, keeping in mind just why she and her family were here. It was Jamalia he was supposed to notice, not her.

'You know what I see here, sire. Out there is Hazibah—the capital—your capital. And there…'

Her voice faltered for a moment then picked up strength as she acknowledged that she could at least speak the truth on this. Here she had nothing to hide.

'There are hundreds of people out there—thousands. Husbands and wives, families and children, all of whom are enjoying the evening—the peace—because of you.'

'Because of me—do you truly think it?'

CHAPTER TWO

THE SOUND HE made was one of obvious scepticism, low and rough in his throat, and it brought her whirling round to face him once again.

'It's true! How can you even doubt it?'

Dear heaven how had he come to be so close? She had barely noticed him move and yet all her senses had been on such high alert that she should have caught even the tiniest movement. But now she was staring him right in the face, eyes burning into eyes, their breaths almost seeming to mingle in the cool of the evening air.

'After all that happened—all you endured...'

She wasn't getting through to him. She might as well be throwing her words at a stone wall for all the impact they made. But she had lived through those times and she knew of the fear that had gripped the country when a rebel group had turned against the young Crown Prince and tried to stage an uprising.

'All that *I* endured?' How could he lace a single syllable with such black cynicism? 'What do you know of it?'

'Doesn't everyone know?'

Even at just thirteen, she had been starkly aware of those shocking television images. The crack of gunfire, the way that everyone had frozen just for a moment. Then security men had rushed forward, some towards the steps of the library where Nabil and his young Queen had been standing, others in the opposite direction in search of the would-be assassin. How could anyone ever forget the image of Nabil sinking to the ground, ignoring the blood streaming from the wound on his left cheek, as he cradled his mortally wounded Queen in protective arms?

Wasn't it this that had kept alive the flame of the torch she had carried for him from the first moment they had met? Even through the long years when he had been so distant, just a remote, untouchable figure glimpsed at one public event or another.

'If you had behaved differently there might have been civil war—worse—but the example you gave when your wife died...'

Now what had she said? She had wanted to express her admiration for him, her respect for the way he had handled a difficult, tragic situation, but instead it was as if she had tossed some bitter acid right in his face. His dark head snapped back, burning eyes narrowing sharply as he turned a shockingly cynical glance in her direction. The cold moonlight caught on the white scar on his cheek, a stark reminder of that terrible day.

'I don't think about it,' he stated flatly. 'I don't want to remember any of that.'

The words were so cold that they slashed at her like a blade of ice but the frightening thing was that at the same time just the simple action of speaking brought him closer to her. The aggressive jut of his jaw was now just inches away from her face, the brilliant glitter of his eyes like polished jet in the moonlight. His powerful body shut out the light from the windows, from the moon, and there was just him, a dark and dangerous shadow looming over her.

She should feel afraid. Common sense screamed at her that she should move hastily away from here, away from him. But, shockingly, something else spread through her body at his nearness, something that held her where she was, unable to move.

It wasn't fear, or even apprehension that fizzed through her veins. No, Aziza had to admit that what she felt was a stinging, burning excitement that was purely and totally feminine and focused tightly on the forceful masculinity of the man before her. The scent of his body surrounded her. She could feel the heat of his skin reach out to her, and that powerful jaw was so close that if she was to lift one hand…

'What the hell…?'

Nabil's snapped response sliced through the air, making her start in shock and realise what she'd done. Impelled by forces that were more potent than rational thought, she had actually put her feelings into action and had stretched out her hand to stroke lightly over the black hairs of his beard, feeling their crisp softness beneath her fingertips.

'What are you doing?'

She should listen to the dangerous note in his voice and heed the warning in it. She was sure she had broken some code of behaviour when in the presence of the Sheikh—and that touching him was positively forbidden—but she couldn't regret it. The feel of his beard against her skin was intoxicating, sending electrical shivers down her nerves. There were grey wings in the glossy black hair, at each side of his head, revealing the way that the passage of time had affected him and there, on the left side of his cheek, was that raised and ridged line of scar tissue, not quite hidden under the luxuriant growth of facial hair. She felt him start and tense as she touched it, and knew a shiver of apprehension, but at the same time those feelings were tangled with a heartfelt sensation of concern and sympathy for the darkness of the memories he had tried to hide behind the words, 'I don't want to remember any of that.'

'I can see why you feel that way.'

The faltering softness of her voice brought his head in closer to catch the words so that now his mouth was just inches above her own. She saw the tightness that had clamped his lips together ease and felt her own mouth soften, lips opening as she tilted her head to one side, feeling the warmth of his breath on her cheek.

'I understand.'

Did he plan to kiss her? The words had barely had time to register in her thoughts before they were pushed away again, driven out by the violence of his response.

'You *understand*?' Nabil demanded in a dark undertone. 'Oh, you do, do you? And what, precisely, is it that you *understand*?'

'I— You...'

Caught up sharp when she was still drifting on the heated waves of awareness that just touching him had brought to the surface, Aziza found the words had tangled up on her tongue and she couldn't get them out. How had she found herself in this situation, here on this darkened terrace with the man who was ruler of all of Rhastaan?

But he was more than a sheikh, he was a man, a dark, powerful male. A man who was like a force of nature, hard and strong as the mountains that bordered his country, and she had overstepped some mark with him, trampling in where angels feared to tread and so sparking off some terrible wave of rejection and fury that she didn't understand.

'What do you know of me? Of anything?'

Nabil moved forward, reaching out to capture her chin in long, powerful fingers, twisting her head so that she was looking up at him, unable to avoid his burning gaze unless she closed her own eyes. Something she didn't dare to do.

'What can you tell me that I don't know already?'

Nabil was having such trouble controlling the force of his feelings that his voice was just a dark, intent hiss of sound. Her words had hit on things he didn't want to remember; things he didn't want to let into his mind. He'd faced them once and it had almost destroyed him. Not again. Not now.

Not when this woman was before him, curvaceous, dark-haired and wide-eyed, reminding him so much of Sharmila. The woman who had died in his arms, taking the bullet that had been meant for him in a bungled assassination attempt. He had felt the impact of that attack in the way she had shuddered in his arms before she had crumpled to the ground. It was only much later that he'd realised that the bullet had nicked his own face, gouging a raw wound along his cheekbone on its way to a much more vulnerable, more valuable target.

But by then he had been unable to care about anything that happened to him because the bullet that had ended his young wife's life had also taken his country's future. The hole her death had left in his own life was something he flinched away from even now. Sharmila had been pregnant with the heir to his throne when she'd died, and the gap that had left in the heart of the country was one he had yet to fill.

Which was why he was going to have to make a decision some time very soon. As everyone kept reminding him. Even Clemmie had advised him, gently of course, that the country desperately needed an heir. He had no time, should have no inclination, for any dalliance with a woman he had just met by chance.

The twist of Zia's head, pulling away from his fingers, dragged Nabil back into the present, and he wasn't any happier to be there. The bitterness of memory lingered, making him tighten his grip, holding her still for a moment.

'You know nothing,' he said, dark and dangerous. 'Nothing at all.'

'I saw...'

'You saw what you wanted to see—what everyone wanted to see. And it has nothing to do with you.'

Her swiftly indrawn breath brought his eyes down to where her soft mouth was partly open, exposing sharp white teeth. As he watched he saw her pink tongue slip out and slick hastily over her dry lips, the tiny gesture making his pulse pound in primal response. Some change in the position of her head brought her face closer to his, the feel of her skin soft against his gripping fingertips.

How did she make him want her so much when he had felt only indifference for so long? The soft sheen of moisture that lingered where her tongue had touched her lips made his own mouth hunger for the taste of her.

One night...

Even as his body put the suggestion into his mind, rational thought was pushing it away again. He was not going down this path again, even if her slender body was pure temptation, the need to hold her close making him ache with the battle against carnal hunger that threatened to destroy rational thought.

'You want me to kiss you, do you?'

He turned his own thoughts against her and felt a

grim satisfaction as he saw the faint start of surprise that revealed the truth of the accusation he had flung at her.

'Is that really what you want? You stupid little fool— you wouldn't even know who you were kissing. What kind of man you wanted...'

A new wave of sound from inside the palace intruded into the dark, private world they had built for themselves out here on the balcony, reminding him once again of his royal duties. He had lingered too long out here, balanced precariously on the edge of self-indulgence. Duty called. The duty he could never escape. It was time he took some much-needed steps away from temptation.

But every male instinct in him rebelled at the thought of leaving her untouched.

'I...'

Aziza had no idea how she could answer him. She had wanted his kiss. How could she deny it when it must have been written on her face, stamped into her eyes? But did she still want it?

Fool that she was, the answer was yes.

And, double fool that she was, he must have seen that truth in her eyes. That hand that was clamped about her chin tightened bruisingly. He pulled her face towards his with a strength she could not resist, and the next moment his mouth came down hard on hers, brutal, ruthless, demanding, but in the same moment shockingly sensual too. White heat flew through her veins, leaving her stunned that she actually didn't go up in flames with the stunning, primitive nature of her unexpectedly wild response. Her legs seemed to melt in the heat, her head spinning in a stunned delirium. With no control over her actions, she opened her lips to his, let him plunder the soft interior of her mouth and met the invasion of his tongue with the dance of her own.

But it was as she gave herself up to his kiss that she felt the sudden change in him, the snatched in breath, the stiffening of his muscular body.

'No...'

With a speed and ruthless determination that made the gesture one of brutal rejection, he snatched his hand away from her face.

'Enough!' he snapped. 'You are dismissed.'

Dismissed?

Who did he think she was? Not Aziza El Afarim, that was for sure. Nabil would never have treated her father's daughter in this way. But then of course this Nabil was not the boy she had known. In his eyes she was nothing more than the maid she had claimed to be, the one who had given her name as Zia. Not 'the beautiful one' but the second El Afarim daughter. The 'spare' to Jamalia's heiress, the problematic one as her father so often reminded her.

So she knew who he was, but this wasn't the Nabil she knew—had thought she knew. This was a harder man, a darker man. Someone she no longer recognised or even wanted to understand.

Someone she no longer wanted to spend any more time with, even if all the cells in her body still burned from the contact that had seared through her.

'Sir.'

It was all she could manage through lips that were as stiff as wood. She'd turned it into a sort of acknowledgement of his command, but she couldn't make her body move away from him, or force her rubbery legs to walk away, as the arrogant lift of his hand, the snap of his fingers, had indicated.

But she didn't need to. Nabil, it seemed, had had enough of this situation. He had no intention of linger-

ing any longer. Instead he had turned on his heel and
was marching towards the doors away from the balcony, this time with her tossed from his mind without
a second thought, his attention firmly on the gathering
back inside the palace. He didn't even spare her a single backward glance.

And for that she could only be thankful. She had
fought to keep her composure and just about managed
it, but now she didn't want Nabil to see the other darker
battle she was having with her innermost self.

Tears burned at the back of her eyes and clogged her
throat, stinging brutally. But she would not let them
fall. Not until Nabil had gone. Not until he had disappeared back into the lighted room in a swish of silken
robes, letting the glazed doors swing to behind him as
they closed against her.

Then at last she bowed her head and gave in to her
feelings, acknowledging the moment of misery as she
admitted the way she felt now. This was not the Nabil
she had adored on sight. Now he was someone else entirely. Another man, a harder, colder being and one she
could never imagine ever wanting to get close to. The
bitter sense of loss was almost more than she could bear.

CHAPTER THREE

'LET IT BE DONE.'

Nabil's own words echoed inside his head as he acknowledged the sweeping bow that his chancellor made before him.

Just four short words and he had set in motion the process that would change his life—and hopefully his country's future—for ever.

Things had moved faster than he had anticipated. He had never thought that he would be here today, ready to take the final step in selecting an arranged bride for himself, less than a month after the tenth anniversary celebrations for Karim and Clemmie. But of course, the traditions and procedures for such an event had been written into the constitution of Rhastaan since the beginnings of time, it seemed, and all he had to do was to speak those four formal words and the whole process swung into action, largely without his involvement.

Until now.

Now it seemed that everyone needed him and his part in the ceremony had suddenly become vital; his opinion, his choice, the only thing that was needed before the process of turning his bride of convenience into the Sheikha of Rhastaan was ready to be finalised.

To be honest, he really didn't give a damn about

this part. After all, hadn't he shown himself to be all sorts of a fool—and a blind fool at that—when it came to choosing women, let alone living with them for the rest of his life, having children…? The much-needed heirs for the kingdom.

Clemmie had talked with him about that just before she'd left.

'Find someone who can take Sharmila's place,' she had said, looking deep into his eyes. 'Someone who can make you happy—give you a family.'

How like Clemmie it was to say it that way. 'A family' was so very different from a woman he married only to provide him and Rhastaan with heirs. A family was what she had with Karim. What he had once thought he had found with Sharmila.

Memory burned as Nabil made himself face the way he had turned away from Clementina Savaneski because she was the bride his parents had chosen for him when he'd been just a child. He had been besotted with Sharmila, believing that in her he had found someone to fill the emptiness in his life. Someone who had wanted him for himself and not on the orders of his dictatorial father. So he had snatched at the excuse offered by the reports of the night Clemmie had spent alone with Karim when the then Crown Prince had been sent to fetch her from where she had fled to England.

Those reports had been slanted by enemies of the state to look far worse than the truth, but he hadn't cared. He'd barely blinked when Clemmie herself had told him that she was in love with someone else. He'd lost a potentially perfect wife—but in doing so he had gained a wonderful friend.

But even to this wonderful friend he had never spoken of the truth of his affair with Sharmila. If he had, then she would never have urged him to find someone who could make him *happy*. That was certainly not the emotion the woman who had once been his Queen now roused in him.

'Sire?' The chancellor had obviously asked some question, was waiting for his reply.

With an effort Nabil dragged his thoughts back to the present and gave a sharp, curt nod of agreement.

'Go ahead,' he declared. 'Put this in motion.'

Another low, sweeping bow and the man left his presence, and Nabil was alone once more. He should be used to it by now. His parents had trained him well, barely sparing more than a moment's attention in their days. It was because of that that Sharmila had had such a pull for him. If only he had known that with her he'd be more alone than at any point in the past ten years. Now, it was how he preferred to be.

Pushing himself to his feet, Nabil walked down to one end, turning to stare down the length of the room towards the raised dais where two heavily carved chairs—two thrones—stood, polished and ornate.

It was a woman to fill one of those thrones, to sit beside him as his Queen, that he was looking for. All he hoped for from this process was a woman who was tolerably attractive and tolerably comfortable to be with.

And fertile.

That was all that he asked his ministers to find for him. And in return he would give her the sort of life most women would dream of. A life of comfort and luxury, jewels, clothing and anything else she asked for. He was sure that one of the women of noble birth his chancellor would deliver to him as arranged would find that acceptable. He was no tyrant. He would give her everything she asked for—within reason. The only thing he couldn't offer was anything that could conceivably be described as love.

He couldn't offer love. That demanded that he also offered his heart. And he didn't have a heart to offer.

So why did his thoughts go to the young woman he had met on the balcony on the night of Karim and Clemmie's anniversary celebrations? His memory filled with images of dark, glistening eyes, black silky hair, a soft voice and that entrancing perfume that had swirled around his senses.

After all that happened—all you went through.

Her words echoed in his thoughts. Her words and the softness of the mouth they fell from—the faint gleam of moisture along her skin where her tongue had slicked over the lower lip. Something raw and needy clawed at his insides, forcing him out of the room and down the corridor at a pace that made his robes sweep against the wall as he moved.

He hadn't seen the woman again that night, though the truth was that he hadn't really tried to find her. He'd had little inclination to seek out the El Afarim clan. He knew, as everyone did, that Farouk El Afarim currently held the balance of power between the crown and the scheming of the rebel leader. If he took his loyalty and that of his own tiny principality to side with Ankhara, then hard-won peace would once again be threatened dangerously.

He knew only too well just how precariously balanced that peace was, and he would do anything to strengthen it. So he knew that El Afaraim's daughter must inevitably be on the list of suitable, acceptable brides for him. To risk seeing Zia in the company of Farouk had been a risk too far, no matter how much the temptation had tugged on his senses.

'No!'

Entering his room, he slammed the door behind him, hearing the heavy thud of the wood with a raw satisfaction at the way it closed off the rest of the world, giving him back the privacy he sought. The only problem was that it would not shut out the thoughts of the girl he had met on the night of the anniversary celebration. Her essence seemed like some sort of persistent shadow, following him wherever he went, whispering in his thoughts at night as he tried to sleep.

He needed to find a wife, as everyone said. No matter if it was the sort of arranged marriage he had rebelled against last time. And look where that had got him. Older, and hopefully wiser, he had decided that this was the only path to follow.

He would do his duty by his country. He would take a wife to be his Queen, to give the kingdom the much-needed heir who would secure the dynasty and guard the peace.

And that was all.

He would be a dutiful king, a faithful husband, surely a caring father. He might not have learned how to be a father from his own coldly distant parents, but surely that meant he knew what not to do? And there was Karim's example to follow.

He needed a wife and he would treat her like a queen. But he would never, ever let her in. If he did she would see that all there was inside him where his heart should be was a cold, empty cavern.

There are hundreds of people out there—thousands. Husbands and wives, families and children, all of whom are enjoying the evening—the peace—because of you.

Zia's voice, low, slightly breathless, sounded so closely in his ear that he almost turned, expecting to see that she had come to stand beside him. But it was nothing but imagination and the forceful impact of the memory of that night.

If he had been able to track her down, then what would have followed? A night of heated passion where he tried to sate this restless hunger in the warmth and softness of her body? Was he really brought so far down that he would have considered using her in this way because she had stirred senses he had thought were dead?

'No!'

She deserved better than that. Better than him.

If nothing else then at least he could tell himself that he had shown a degree of honour when he had turned his back on her even though it was obvious that she had felt that same dangerous tug of attraction. He had spared her the moment when he would have had to walk away from her after one night. Because one night was all they could have had. He had already decided that he would speak those words and set in motion the search for a suitable wife and Queen.

'Let it be done.'

And now things were moving forward. The news the chancellor had brought to him today was that matters had been set in hand. Prospective brides had been chosen, their families approached. All that mattered now was for him to see them. To make his choice.

'Choice!'

He uttered the word aloud like a dark curse as he stared out of the window.

The truth was that he would have more personal choice of a new horse or even a hunting dog. The facts were that it was being made clear that he must choose on the basis of politics and diplomacy; the benefits to the country that his wife would bring, rather than anything else. Left to his *choice*, he would not go through this at all.

But he had vowed to do his duty to his country, and that vow held him like a chain.

'But you don't need me to be there!' Aziza protested, turning to face her sister so that the determination on her face must show as clearly as possible. She had no need to try and show her horror; it must be evident from her tone and her expression. 'This has nothing to do with me! It's—it's you they have asked for.'

'I know.'

Jamalia's smile had just a hint of smugness in it, and as she glanced in the huge mirror on the wall she positively preened as she smoothed back a non-existent loose hair in her sleek black mane. But a moment later her self-control slipped just a bit, showing a touch of vulnerability beneath.

'But… I can't go alone. I'll need someone to help me—dress me—a chaperone.'

'But why does it have to be me?'

Why couldn't it be anyone else? Jamalia's maid? Some other attendant? If only their mother hadn't taken ill at just this particular moment. Now when she needed it least there slid into Aziza's memory the recollection of how she had claimed to be just that—Jamalia's maid— that night on the terrace when she had come up against Nabil in the shadows of the night.

'I don't understand you.' Jamalia's frown was a mix- ture of disbelief and displeasure. 'I would have thought that you would look forward to another trip to the cap- ital. You enjoyed the anniversary celebration, didn't you?'

Aziza made a sort of inarticulate sound that her sister could take as agreement if she wanted to. Enjoyment wasn't a part of the way she looked back on the night on the balcony when she had met up again with the man who had once held such a huge place in her young heart.

How could he have changed so much in the ten years since she had last seen him? Or had he changed at all? Wasn't it more likely that she had been the one who had changed? She had grown up, matured, and that had meant that she no longer saw through the eyes of a child. Instead she saw the truth about the man behind her childish crush. Nabil was no different from the lordly boy who had occasionally enchanted her with a careless smile. It was just that she had never seen the truth before.

He hadn't even recognised her! But something in her had recognised what he was. All that was male and virile in him had spoken very clearly to her most feminine core. She still got the shivers inside at just the thought.

'Are you sure you want to go at all?'

She knew it was the wrong question but she had to ask it. Diplomacy, politics, the uneasy truce between two warring factions demanded that the Sheikh had a wife, and Jamalia was a prime candidate to fill that role. That was why they had been at the anniversary celebrations, after all, in the hope that Jamalia would catch Nabil's eye. But Jamalia and their parents hadn't met up with Nabil that night.

Aziza had and, recalling the cold, bitter man she had talked with, she was now forced to wonder, could she watch her sister marry that man?

Nabil had been so changed from the boy she'd given her heart to when she was young, and her heart ached for the loss of the person she thought he'd been. She could have watched Jamalia marry that Nabil…or could she? Wouldn't that have broken her heart in a very different way? Loving Nabil as she had, wouldn't she have longed for him as her own?

So could she go with her sister—watch her perhaps be chosen—watch her marry the Nabil she knew existed now?

'Do I want to? Of course I want to go. Think of it, Aziza—to marry Nabil…become the Sheikha…' Jamalia's eyes glowed at the thought. 'The clothes…the jewels…'

'Is that all?'

'All?' Jamalia shook her head in disbelief. 'It means a lot—and of course there is the added advantage of the fact that Sheikh Nabil is such a gorgeous man!'

She shivered in delighted anticipation. A couple of days before, Aziza might not have recognised the full impact of her response but now it brought back echoes of the way she had felt on a moonlit night on the balcony of the Ashar palace. Even now, just thinking of it, her blood heated and tiny, stinging sensations of awareness prickled over her skin.

'Besides, you have to be my chaperone. Papa says so.'

And if Papa said so then that was it, Aziza acknowledged. His word was law and there was no going against it. The thought of facing her father's wrath if she denied his command was actually worse than the prospect of meeting up with Nabil again.

'So will you come?'

There was no other answer she could give. She wouldn't have to see Nabil. There was no reason for her to have any contact with him.

'All right, then. Yes, I'll come.'

CHAPTER FOUR

NABIL HAD HAD ENOUGH. He had thought that by agreeing to an arranged marriage he was going to make things easier. That all he had to do was to instruct his chancellor to find a suitable bride, agree to any terms her family proposed and proceed to the wedding ceremony. Now it seemed that the rituals and procedures would never end. Today he had expected to see the chosen candidates; pick one to become his wife. Instead he was weighing up possible treaties, the balance needed for peace.

Could this thing get more like a bidding war? His breath hissed in through his teeth as he tried to find the patience to listen to what Omar was now telling him. Had he spent the last ten years dragging the country into the present century only to find that his need for a wife would take it right back again to the dark ages it had been in when his father had ruled?

'I understand,' he said at last, driven to the end of his patience. 'Give me the list.'

An impatient gesture of his outstretched hand brought the chancellor hurrying, passing the sheet of paper to him. One name jumped out at him at once, and he knew there had never been a choice. Not really. This had been inevitable from the moment he had put the bride search into motion. There might have been other names, but those had really had no weight to their candidacy. If he *really* wanted to secure the throne, to ensure peace, then there was only this one way he could go.

Jamalia; Farouk El Afarim's eldest daughter.

Just a maid. I am with Jamalia.

Damn you, Zia, get out of my head! He needed to think clearly and with the image of the woman he'd met on the balcony haunting his thoughts, that was impossible. But it didn't take much thought to know that an alliance with the El Afarims was the most valuable gift he could give to Rhastaan.

'Is Jamalia here today?'

'She is sire but...'

'I will see her.'

A sound the older man made brought his head up fast. He could almost feel the force of his own glare reflected back at him from Omar's eyes.

'I will see her—and no one else. I know that it isn't *protocol*—' he emphasised the word sardonically '—for me to meet her as yet. But surely there must be some way I can see her without having to come face to face?'

'There is a room—with a two-way mirror.'

'That will do.'

'Oh, Zia, why do you think we're here? What is happening?'

'How should I know?'

Aziza regretted the sharpness of her words as soon as they'd escaped her. She didn't feel quite in control of her tongue, or her thoughts. She had been a bundle of nerves ever since they had set out on this second visit to the palace. If she thought she'd been apprehensive before at the thought of meeting Nabil again, now that she knew the sort of mature, powerfully sexy man he had become, just the thought of being in the same building as him tied her stomach in knots. Now this new development, the way they had been told to move to this room and wait, set her nerves on edge, making it difficult to breathe.

'I'm sorry—but obviously I know no more than you.'

Jamalia was in a twitchy enough state as it was. Aziza wasn't going to let on that she had her strong suspicions that the large mirror on the wall in which her sister was preening herself was in fact a window through which they could be observed by anyone who wanted to watch.

'My hair's a mess!' Jamalia tugged at a lock of silky black hair, twisting it round her fingers as she made a petulant face at her reflection. 'I knew I should have got you to do it instead of—'

'Shall I do it now?' Aziza volunteered hastily. Anything to distract her sister.

Dressing Jamalia's hair was a skill she had learned from a very young age. She had hoped that if she made her father's favourite look good then it might win her some of Farouk's approval. That hadn't worked, but at least Jamalia appreciated her efforts.

'It won't take a moment to braid these pieces, fasten them up at the sides.'

'All right.' Jamalia's petulant expression eased as she watched her younger sister set to work on her hair. 'Hmm—that doesn't look half bad. And I tell you what would make it look even better…'

She was fumbling with her necklace as she spoke, never taking her eyes from the mirror as she lifted the necklace and placed it on her head.

'Help me fasten it, Zia…'

In a moment, the heavy jewelled pendant was hanging in the centre of her forehead, right against the silky black of her hair.

'See?' Jamalia preened, turning her head to see the effect from both sides, smiling at herself—and possibly at their hidden viewer—as she did so. 'The perfect look for the new Sheikha!'

It must be wonderful to have her sister's total self-confidence, Aziza thought as she compared their two images in the mirror. But then Jamalia had always known she was beautiful, always been treated as the jewel in the family. Jamalia took after their father: tall, slender, elegant, stunning. They were so alike, it was no wonder Farouk had always favoured her. Beside her glamourous sibling Aziza felt like a small, rounded puppy, cuddly perhaps, but lacking the sort of pedigree Jamalia wore effortlessly. Because of that, it had always been made plain to her that it would cost her family an expensive dowry to marry her off.

You want me to kiss you, do you...? From the depths of her memory came the sound of Sheikh Nabil's voice, dark with mockery and contempt, so clearly that she could almost believe he had come into the room behind them. *You stupid little fool—you wouldn't even know who you were kissing. What kind of man you wanted...*

Did Jamalia know what sort of a husband she would get in this man? Did she understand—or did she even care? It seemed that all her sister cared about was the title of Sheikha, the ceremonial role, the wealth and luxury that would come with it. At least her sister wouldn't be pushed into a totally subservient place as Nabil's wife, as might have happened in the past. In the ten years since his first wife had died, the Sheikh had worked ceaselessly it seemed to ensure that women had a better life, more equality. Hadn't she longed to take advantage of it herself, to be able to go to university to study languages? Another mark against her, in her father's opinion. After all, who would want to marry a bluestocking, someone who spent so much of her free time with her books? At least she'd learned to drive and enjoy the independence that gave her, while her sister had never bothered to take driving lessons.

But then of course, if she became Queen, Jamalia would never need to steer her own vehicle. She would have a sleek, luxurious, armour-plated official car at her disposal, together with a professional chauffeur, on duty day or night, whenever she wanted him.

Jamalia as Queen… Why did her stomach seem to drop, her nerves clench, at just the thought? Not at the thought of her sister as Sheikha—but as Nabil's wife.

'That is the woman you mean?'

Nabil was already turning away from the two-way mirror through which he had been observing the two women in the room beyond them. He had seen enough. If the truth was told he had seen more than he had ever wanted or expected.

He had never anticipated that he would see *her*. That the woman who had plagued his thoughts would be there in the room with his prospective bride. Well, of course he had known that this Zia was Jamalia's maid. She had said so herself. But he hadn't known that Zia would be here, now, with Jamalia when he had come to see her today. He had expected Jamalia's mother to be acting as chaperone and instead had found himself staring straight at Zia.

And that had thrown everything off-balance.

It had forced him to remember the heavy throb of his blood when he had been talking with Zia on the balcony. The way that the soft scent of her skin, mixed with some light floral fragrance, had drifted towards him on the night air, making him think of the secrecy of a bedroom, soft sheets…

Damn it to hell! Even now he was thinking of her—of Zia—when she should be the last thing on his mind. Perhaps he should have taken her to bed on that night—when she had been practically begging him to do so—and got this sensual itch out of his system.

'Sire?' Omar was waiting for him to continue. 'And she is the woman of your choice?'

'She…' This was getting worse. He'd almost said yes to Omar's selection of a bride when his mind had been full of some other woman. Of bedding his prospective bride's maid.

Clearing his thoughts with a brutal shake of his head, he brought his mind back into focus.

'No. No, she's not.'

How could he ever marry Jamalia when as his Queen she would surely bring her maid with her? And yet how could he now refuse to take Jamalia as his wife and risk insulting her father by rejecting his beautiful daughter?

He could see why Jamalia had been selected. She was stunning; there was no doubt about that. She would look magnificent as Queen. But he wanted more than a queen, someone who would give him an heir to his throne. He also wanted someone who would be a mother to his children. He hadn't acknowledged how much that mattered to him until now. Until he had seen Jamalia preening in the mirror, her total sense of entitlement reminding him of nothing so much as his own mother.

Having been the child of a woman who loved her role as Queen so much that she had never had time for her son, he never wanted any child of his to go through that. He had seen his parents for perhaps an hour or less each week. Times when he had been brought from the nursery, spruced up and groomed, ready for the formal occasion that spending time with his mother had always been. Brought into her private sitting room, he'd had to bow the requisite three times before he could even approach her. And he had always known that the delicate touch of her hand on his head as she commented on how he had grown was one of the two gestures of 'affection' she would allow him.

The other was when his brief time was up and his nurse had prepared to escort him from the room. Then his mother would bend her head towards him, wreathing him in the overpowering scent of her perfume, and offer him her powdered cheek for his kiss, allowing him only the lightest, briefest, moment of contact for fear that the contact might smudge her immaculate make-up.

And then he was dismissed.

Small wonder then that the death of both his mother and father in the helicopter crash had barely touched him. How could he miss people who had created him but yet had been barely present in his life? The death of his old nurse, two years later when he was sixteen, had had a far more dramatic effect on his life.

That was not how he wanted the future to be for his children. Having seen how Clemmie was with her son and daughter, he wanted that sort of mothering for any child of his. And something about Jamalia's self-absorption scraped over his skin like sandpaper.

'No?'

Clearly Omar thought he had lost his mind—or at least come close to it. But the truth was that he felt more clearer-headed than he had in a long time.

'But, sire—the treaty...'

He didn't need reminding about the importance of the treaty, but now, remembering the time he had spent in Farouk's home when he'd been twelve, he also knew why, unconsciously, he had been avoiding all contact with the man's older daughter. Told that he was spending some time with an important family, his mind had caught on the word *family*, hoping that there might be someone who might become a friend. Or that the El Afarims could at least show him something of what a family life might mean.

Instead, it had been plain that the visit was more one of diplomacy and state. Even then, there'd been obviously plenty of scheming going on in the background, as the way that Jamalia had been pushed forward from the start had made plain. He had never taken to the elder El Afarim daughter but…

'There is a younger sister, isn't there?'

He had no idea where the memory had come from but suddenly it was clear in his mind. The image of a small, shy child who had peered out at him from behind her mother's skirts, a soft giggle escaping her curved lips. A little girl so much shorter and more rounded than her older sister with the smile of an angel that had made him feel welcome in a moment. A girl who had cared for a bundle of orphaned kittens as if they were precious to her, feeding them from a dropper with infinite patience, and who, young as she had been, had had a magic touch with a crying baby cousin, soothing him to sleep in just moments. If he had to make an arranged marriage to provide heirs for the sake of his country's future then the least he could do was to give those heirs a mother who would give them more than he had ever had.

'If the treaty is to go ahead, then all it needs is that I marry one of the El Afarim girls?'

'Indeed, but...'

'But nothing.' Nabil's hand came up to cut off any further conversation with a slicing gesture. 'Enough. If the treaty still stands, then that's the way it will be. If I have to have an arranged wife, then I'll take the younger sister. Let it be done.'

CHAPTER FIVE

How could your life turn inside out in the space of just a few days, not even a month? Aziza wondered to herself as she stood, waiting for the door of the banqueting hall to open, and for her walk—surely the longest walk on earth—to begin. She had barely been aware of each day that had passed, all of them filled with frantic organisation, fittings, meetings, all the arrangements that were needed to turn her into the Sheikh's chosen bride.

The Sheikh's chosen bride.

There they were, the four words that had taken her life as she'd known it and shattered it into a million tiny fragments that could never be made whole again. The words were so shocking, so unbelievable, that they made her grab hold of her father's arm, holding on tightly for fear that her legs might give way beneath her.

The rich golden silk of her ceremonial robes, heavy with embroidery, weighed down on her, making her feel as if she was carrying a burden on her shoulders, and the layers of the veil she wore clung around her face until it was almost impossible to breathe, obscuring her sight so that she had to rely on her father's support to move forward and walk straight to the right place.

'Steady…' her father urged as she swayed slightly, hesitating nervously.

If anything brought home the change in her situation, it was that. The fact that her father had spoken to soothe her, instead of the sharp reproach she would have expected in the past. She was someone new now, and Farouk's attitude had had to change along with her life.

'Remember, he chose you.'

He chose you. She still couldn't believe that those words were true. That they had actually been said in the moment that her father had come to find her and Jamalia in the room where they had been waiting, all day it seemed, for some sort of announcement on Sheikh Nabil's selection of a bride. They had known that something had happened when Farouk had arrived, his mouth seemingly clamped tight on the news he had to deliver and his dark eyes burning with a suppressed excitement until he'd been free to speak openly.

'Sheikh Nabil has made his decision,' he had said and immediately Aziza's eyes had gone to her sister who had pushed herself out of her chair, hectic colour flooding her cheeks. The 'diadem' she had created out of her necklace still glittered on her forehead like an omen.

But it was towards his younger daughter that Farouk had turned, his own smile slightly uneven. He had not been able to supress his delight that one of his daughters was to become the Sheikh's bride, but was bemused that it was Aziza and not his 'jewel', her elder sister.

'He chose you.'

Aziza struggled to breathe naturally, making herself draw in air, then let it out again, fighting to steady the way that her feet hit the ground as she moved forward again. The marble floor felt disturbingly uneven beneath the soles of her silk slippers and she could barely focus through the layer upon layer of golden gauze that formed her veil to see the man standing at the far end of the hall.

Nabil—her husband-to-be!—was just a blur of white in his full ceremonial robes, the *gutra* on his head, bound, with a gold *igal*, acting like a blind, hiding his face from her.

But that was how it was supposed to be in this ceremony. Aziza knew that both she and Nabil were meant to be just symbols—the ruler and his consort. Not a man and a woman. Because this arranged marriage was for the sake of the country.

That was one of the reasons why she had not been able to refuse to go through with this. *For the sake of the country* had been drilled into her from the moment she had been told that she was Nabil's choice. The vital treaties that had been built around their proposed union could be destroyed if she tried to back out. She was not supposed to be a person, just a bargaining tool. No one thought of her hopes, her dreams, her feelings. Anything like that was supposed to be buried under the overwhelming pride of being the Sheikh's prospective bride. That was why she had this new-found approval from her father. She was the chosen one.

He chose you.

No one—not even Aziza herself—had reckoned with the memories she carried from her childhood, the ardent crush she had had on Nabil from a very early age. That had grown as she'd watched him leave youth behind and turn into a man who had endured loss and betrayal and now had put them behind him.

But who was Nabil now? Were her memories of him just the fantasies of a child, or did they have any foundation in the truth? In her dreams he had always been the man she would marry—but those dreams were just fantasy. She had never dreamed of the hard, cold man she had met that night on the balcony.

And yet it seemed she couldn't let go of the girlhood yearnings. She had wept for her disillusionment that night, but in the moment that her father had told her that she was the Sheikh's chosen bride all those dreams had come rushing back, bringing with them new hopes, new hungers, that her younger self would never even have been able to imagine.

She *wanted* to be the chosen one. Whether she was Zia the maid, or Aziza the second-best daughter, she longed to be special to someone. And Nabil had seen her; in that room with the two-way mirror, he had seen her with Jamalia and he had chosen her.

She was at Nabil's side now, her right hand lifted from her father's arm and placed into his, her small fingers almost swallowed up in the length and strength of his palm.

And there it was again. That stinging, fizzing, burning rage of response that his touch stirred, making her snatch in a breath, unable to control the race of her heart.

It was how it had happened on the balcony, the night of the anniversary celebrations.

Now, just being so close to him, had brought back all the feelings that had threatened to burn her alive that night on the balcony. Even through the concealing folds of the veils, his black gaze burned into her skin, branding her, marking her as his.

She wanted that. She wanted this man as she had never wanted any other human being in her life. She wanted those childhood reveries to come true. Oh, she knew that there was no way the dreams of Nabil she had had then could ever become reality. The adult male Nabil she had met on the balcony was light years away from her childhood hero. She knew that he was harsh now. A hard man, devoid of any warm emotion. She blushed to remember his refusal to kiss her that night. She should resist this union. But her foolish heart wouldn't listen to reason.

Somehow she got through the ceremony, led into the responses, the words she needed to say, guided by the celebrant. She accepted the ring that Nabil pushed on to her finger and then turned, her hand on *her husband's* arm, and made her way back down the room. There was a huge change in the atmosphere, in the attitude of everyone present. She was no longer even the chosen one but actually the Sheikh's wife.

The greatest shock came when she saw her mother sweep into a low curtsey and her father—her *father*!— bow respectfully as she passed. It was then that it hit home to her that this marriage had changed so much for her personally as well as for the country.

She was no longer second to anyone—except of course Nabil, her husband. Her days of being the 'other daughter', the one who was usually kept in the background, were over. Most of all she no longer had to obey her father, subject everything she did to his scrutiny. She was free.

Or was she? She had put her life and her future—her body too—into the hands of the man who was walking beside her. That grip on her fingers was very firm, his skin warm and hard against her own. It made her shiver inside to feel it and the twist of nerves low down in her body forced her to think of what it might be like to have those hands on other more intimate parts of her body. She had blundered into this in a blind bewilderment, half-influenced by the yearning she had felt as a child, half-reaching for the freedom she thought this marriage would offer, clinging on to the knowledge that Nabil was a reformer, had taken an interest in improving the lives of women in his country. So different from her father's oppressive and traditional views on women. But was that freedom possible at all or had she just exchanged one form of slavery for another?

She drifted through the feasting and celebrations that followed the wedding as if in some sort of delirium, a feeling that was only increased by being hidden behind the concealing curtain of her veils. If she wanted to eat, she would have to slip the food under those curtains in order to reach her mouth.

But the reality was that she couldn't eat a thing, just pushed the rich, spicy food around on the gold surface of her plate, unable to think of swallowing a morsel. Beside her Nabil sat, his hand resting on the arms of his chair, his long body seeming relaxed in his seat. But this close to him she couldn't be unaware of the way that those deep, dark eyes watched the room, noting every movement. The wary alertness bothered her.

'Sire...'

Her voice, dry with apprehension, croaked slightly as the sound pulled his head round, black eyes seeming to sear through the concealing veil and on to her face.

'My name is Nabil,' he said softly enough but with an edge to his own name that brought her up sharp. Her eyes drawn to the sudden movement of one long, bronzed hand, she saw how those strong fingers had clenched over the gold fork that lay beside his plate. A plate that he had barely touched either. Suddenly she was stingingly aware of the fact that his given name was one so very few people had the right to use. In his position as the head of government, the ruler of Rhastaan, he was the Sheikh, the King, His Highness—but how few people could call him just *Nabil*.

And suddenly, from the mists of bitter memory, she had an unwanted recollection of the shocking scenes played out on the televisions sets of the country ten years before. In the deafening silence of the aftermath of the assassination attempt, Nabil, his own face marked with the blood of the glancing wound he had suffered, had bent over the fallen body of Sharmila, his pregnant Queen. As he'd lowered his head to hers, it had been possible to see how her lips had moved to silently form one word: Nabil.

'N-Nabil…' she tried hesitantly, wanting to reach out and touch her fingers to that hand so tightly clamped around his fork. But it seemed as if a force field of distance, of rejection, shimmered around him, and instead she clenched her own hands in her lap, fearful of shattering the atmosphere with a dangerous move.

Nabil made his fingers ease their hold on the fork he held. Now was not the time to think of how many years it had been since he had heard a woman—other than Clementina—use his name in that way. Nor to recognise how those damned veils muffled everything about her voice so that it could come from any female, old or young. It seemed so strange that the only image he had of the woman who was now his wife was the image of her as a girl that had pushed him into a decision that might just turn out to be as foolish and rash as the one that had made him take Sharmila as his first wife. But at least this decision had been made with his head, not the rush of desire and loneliness that had pushed him into Sharmila's arms.

Or the one that had had him actually considering taking Aziza's sister's maid to bed.

Damn it, no! He had let Zia creep into his mind at exactly the point he should not be thinking of her. His focus should be on his bride—on Aziza.

An Aziza who was obviously no longer a child. She had blossomed—physically at least. That slender body was still all woman, high, firm breasts and gently curving hips, but her face was totally concealed behind the veils that tradition demanded, frustrating any attempt to actually see what she looked like. He knew her sister was the reputed beauty but surely Aziza couldn't have lost all the angelic prettiness that he remembered? All those years ago, she had been the one who had treated him like a person, not as a potential king, marked out by the role that was all Jamalia and her parents seemed to see. She had giggled when he'd spotted her stealing sweetmeats, pressed a finger to her lips to warn him not to betray her. And that smile…

Silently Nabil cursed the tradition of the golden bridal veil. If only he could see through that damned gauze—see his wife!

Burning with frustration, he gave up trying to penetrate the material that concealed Aziza's face and let his gaze drop abruptly to look down at her still full dish.

'You are not eating.'

To Aziza's ears it sounded like an accusation, a reproof.

'I—I'm not hungry.'

To her amazement a corner of Nabil's mouth quirked up into a sudden and unexpected smile at her response.

'That is not like the Aziza I remember.'

'You—remember?' It hit her hard in her stomach, her mind reeling in shock to think that he recalled her at all.

'You stole the candied fruits from the table,' he told her. 'I remember wondering how you could get away with that when you were barely tall enough to see over the top of it.'

'I took them for my nurse!' Aziza answered sharply, discomforted at the thought that he recalled her as only a greedy little girl. She wanted him to think of her as a woman. The woman he had chosen. The woman he wanted.

'Of course you did.'

When he laughed like that she felt that she might melt, slipping from her chair to lie in a pool at his feet. It seemed impossible to believe that this gorgeous, sexy male could be interested in her at all. And yet he'd had the chance to marry her sister...

Realisation was like a shock to her heart, snatching away her breath so that she was grateful for the fact that the veil hid so much from those burning black eyes. If he had seen her and Jamalia together, then he must know that she was the Zia who had claimed to be only his sister's maid. He'd seen her, recognised her and still chosen her. It made her head spin to think of it and more than ever before she cursed the masking of the veil that meant she had no hope of reading what was really in those glittering dark eyes.

'Do you still like sweetmeats?'

A change had come over Nabil's voice. It had deepened, taking on a husky edge, and those dark eyes were searching the table, looking for something. A moment later he was leaning forward, waving away the attentions of the servant as he pulled a polished dish of sugar-coated grapes and dates towards him. Picking up a luscious-looking grape, he held it out towards her temptingly.

'Try this.'

It wasn't the sweet treat that was tempting, Aziza

reflected as she felt the noise and the colour of her surroundings fade away until there was just her and Nabil and the glistening green of the fruit between them. Her mouth was watering but not with the need to taste the fruit.

'Here...'

Before she was aware of what he had planned, he had leaned closer, using his free hand to lift the side of the veil and slipping his fingers in to lift the grape to her mouth, pressing it softly against her lips.

'Taste.'

She couldn't do anything but respond as he said. Her eyes fixed on him through the veil, she let her mouth fall open, took in the grape and bit into it. Fresh, crisp juice flooded her mouth, contrasting with the delicate dusting of spiced sugar.

'Good?'

Aziza could only pray that he would catch the tiny nod of her head that was all she was capable of. Savouring the delicate mouthful, she chewed slowly, swallowed and immediately wished for...

'More?' He seemed to be able to read her mind, moving the remainder of the grape so that it rested against her mouth.

Nabil could feel her soft skin, the warmth of her breath on the fingers that held the grape, but he wished to hell that he could see her face and know exactly who he had married.

She was nothing but a blur behind the damned veil. Dark hair, dark pools of eyes. But then those were what he recalled from the hazy memories of all those years ago. She had to have changed...

Who the hell would have thought that cuddly, sweet-natured Aziza would have turned into a subtle sex kitten in the years since he had seen her last?

He wanted to touch, let the fingers that had lifted the side of the veil brush against the downy silk of her skin. But as he leaned forward and she turned towards him his senses were suddenly assailed by a waft of scent that reached out to him.

Hauntingly familiar.

Shockingly familiar.

It made his whole body freeze, realisation kicking him hard in the gut. He knew that perfume. Sandalwood and jasmine. It was a scent he associated with one woman only. Zia.

Since when did a maid wear the same perfume as her mistress?

Unless...

Had all the lights been turned out or could he really not see even if he blinked hard? Her face was hidden, just a blur behind the veil, but even if that obstacle had been tossed aside he would still be fighting to clear his vision. Had he walked into the same trap as before? *Married* into the same set-up as with Sharmila? Had he really been deceived once more by a pretty face, a seductive body?

Who the hell was she?

Nabil had suddenly gone so still that Aziza felt as if everything and everyone else had evaporated, leaving them in an intense vacuum where there was only the two of them, and the shimmering haze of awareness that was building with every breath she took. Her senses swam in sensual overload as she caught the scent of his skin so close to her nostrils. The hand that held up the veil on the other side was warm and gentle, long fingers slightly calloused from the controlling grip on the reins of the wild Arabian stallions he loved to ride. Once again the thought of those hands on her body, removing her *djbella*, dropping it to the floor, those tiny calluses catching on the smoothness of her skin, made her burn between her legs, her mouth drying in the rush of heated awareness. So much so that she snatched at the second half of the grape he was offering her, misjudging the action so that her mouth closed around not just the fruit but also the warm, tanned fingers that were holding it to her mouth.

Oh, dear lord! The words of panic pounded inside her head as she waited to see the way he would snatch his hand away in anger at her clumsiness.

It didn't happen. Only that total silent, shocking stillness.

All she wanted was to bring him out of it. To make him move, speak—*smile* if she could.

Emboldened by the fizz of excitement that bubbled through her veins, she let her tongue slip against his fingers, tasting his clean skin and the slightly musky tang that turned her insides molten.

'Aziza…'

She had heard that note, half-groan, half-laughter, in his voice before. On the balcony. Then he had rejected her, turned and walked away from her. But today there was no room for rejection or dismissal here. She was his. She was his Queen and her head spun in the delirium that combined with the heated rush of excitement and purely feminine need she was experiencing, turning her head.

She wanted to see that response again. But more than that she wanted the taste of him on her tongue again. Hunger made her bolder, slicking away the sugary taste of the grapes and replacing it with the stronger, more basic taste of warm male skin as she swirled her tongue around those strong fingers, resting her cheek against the warmth and hardness of his other hand as she did so.

'Aziza!' This time it was a very different sound. The groan might still be there but every trace of the laughter had vanished, leaving his voice hard and clipped even though it was never raised above the level of a whisper. 'Enough, lady!'

It was like being slapped in the face, jolted back into reality with a nerve-jangling rush. He pulled his hands away from her face, letting her head drop to one side as he snatched his fingers away from her mouth, the heavy gold ring he wore on his finger—his wedding finger—catching on the fine gauze of her veil so that it tugged sharply against the points where it was fastened into the ornate style of her hair, bringing tears to her eyes.

Nabil had slammed to his feet, silencing everyone around them. All conversation stopped, every head turned their way, and the hushed atmosphere suddenly felt cold and oppressive, a sensation that was made worse by the way that Nabil now towered over her, his tall, powerful frame blocking out the light from the candles.

'Enough,' he said again and her mind was whirling too hard, too fearfully to be able to put any interpretation on his tone this time. She had overstepped some invisible line that she hadn't even known was drawn between them, and she didn't know which way to react.

If she had needed any proof of how commanding, how powerful he was, then it was there in the absolute stillness of every person in the hall following that single word. The total silence as they waited for him to move, to speak again. But then he didn't need to speak, or raise his voice in command. No one could ever have questioned the sheer force of nature that was Nabil bin Rashid Al Sharifa as he stood, tall and proud beside her, holding out his hand to her. No words, just the silence of command. A command she would be every sort of a fool to try to resist.

Slowly she put her hand into his, felt herself pulled to her feet with such force that she fell against the rock-hard strength of Nabil's body, losing her breath in a gasp of reaction.

'We're out of here.'

That was the quick, dark mutter he uttered against her ear, the rest of his attention directed out into the huge hall.

'My bride is tired…'

That was what he told their audience, all of whom seemed transfixed by this unexpected development, the suddenness of the change in his mood that went against all the ceremony and ritual that was planned.

'I'm not…' she managed on a croak but just a turn of his head in her direction silenced the rest. He hauled her even closer to him, the pressure of his arms crushing her against the hard heat of him.

'We will leave…'

At the end of the hallway a door that had been left open suddenly slammed back hard into its frame, the resulting bang startling everyone and silencing Nabil abruptly. Aziza was astonished to feel the way his strong body jerked against hers, the sudden tension in that long spine. For a moment he was completely still, bringing her own heartbeat to a halt as she wondered just what had changed his mood.

'Nabil…'

But then it seemed that his thoughts returned to the present and he lifted his head again.

It had all happened in too short a space of time for anyone else to notice, Aziza realised as she saw no echo of her own confusion on the faces of their audience of guests.

'My wife and I are leaving now,' he continued, ignoring her own bewilderment so completely that she felt she must have been mistaken; that the abrupt change of mood had never happened. 'But please, continue the celebrations…'

And that was it—he was turning, heading for the door. Aziza had no choice but to go with him because she was still clamped tight against him, the strength of his arms half-walking, half-carrying her out of the banqueting hall and along the marble corridors away from the ceremonial part of the palace, towards the private, personal area.

Had she done something wrong? Aziza didn't know if it was fear or excitement that buzzed along every nerve, making her blood pound at the base of her skull so that she was sure Nabil must see it. How could he miss the throbbing pulse in her throat that revealed the race of her heart from underneath her skin?

She was held so tightly that there was no chance to break away if she wanted to. But did she want to? What she really felt was a very sensual, very feminine need to continue to be held this way. To be imprisoned in the arms of this powerful man.

And she had thought that now she would be freer! That this marriage would win her a new liberty; a chance to be herself, no longer subject to her father's tyrannical will. But, if there was one thing that this hasty, determined departure from the formal celebration of their wedding had shown her, it was that the only thing that had changed was that she was no longer subject to her father's rules—but instead bound by what her husband demanded of her. And when Nabil decided on something there was no chance at all that she could say no. What he wanted, he got. But what was it that he wanted now?

She had been so fearful that she had put a foot wrong that any other answer never occurred to her. It was only when Nabil flicked a hand in another autocratic gesture towards the attendants who dogged their footsteps that a flash of insight, like a fork of lighting, came from the back of her mind to illuminate her thoughts and leave her shaking in apprehension in a new and very different way. This was not about doing something wrong. It was about something deeper, darker, much more primitive. It was about the most basic connection between a man and a woman.

'Nothing at all.' Nabil stated inflexibly. 'Leave us! My wife and I want to be alone.'

My wife and I...

The full truth dawned in the moment that Nabil swung her round into a new corridor, dragging her with him, kicking the heavy carved door into place behind them and making a rough sound of satisfaction as it slammed fast.

And it was that sound, so very different from the way he had reacted when the door had slammed in the banqueting hall, that told its own story and left Aziza in no doubt as to what was happening, and why she was here.

Nabil wanted to be alone with his wife...and, for better or worse, she was that wife.

CHAPTER SIX

Nabil felt as if he was on fire. He was surprised that there hadn't been a trail of scorch marks along the floor to mark their progress from the banqueting hall to his private apartments. It was as if he had come alive after ten long years in the dark and he was so hot and hungry that he felt it was about to cause an explosion. He wanted; he ached. And yet he knew that the ending to this night was never going to be the one that he had anticipated earlier.

With the door closed safely between them and his overly attentive servants, he slammed to a halt, swinging Aziza round so that she thudded up against him, the softness of her body colliding with the hardness of his.

And that was a near-fatal mistake because it set his pulse rate into overdrive. The pressure of her breasts crushed against his chest, the scent of her skin and her hair and the way it felt to know the heat and hardness of his arousal cradled in the bowl of her hips made his head swim in sexual need.

Which warned him how right he had been to worry. That all was not as it seemed. Because how the hell could he feel this newly awakened hunger for two women—Aziza and the maid—in such a short time? He knew what the guests at the wedding thought about their precipitous departure. Hell, he wanted them to be right. Wanted them to think that he had thoughts only of taking his wife to bed and setting about the process of creating an heir. But they didn't know that he'd been here once before. And barely escaped with his life.

He didn't know what had stayed his hand at the banquet. What had stopped him from wrenching up her veil and exposing the truth to everyone there? The political implications if he was right. The fact that he wasn't sure. And the thought of doing that to his new bride, to Aziza, if that was truly who she was.

But how was he supposed to *think* when his mind was wiped clean of anything but the hardness of his body and the hunger that was such a brutal physical need?

She'd come with him easily enough, turning at the tug of his hand on hers, her feet in the jewelled slippers moving silently down the corridor. He couldn't let her go; he held her crushed up against his side where she was small enough to be slotted underneath his armpit, her head resting against his shoulder, his left arm curved round her ribcage, left hand just below the swell of her left breast. With every movement he could feel the sway of her bosom, the heat from it seeming to burn into his skin. He wanted more—more contact—more of her. But at the same moment he wished she was anywhere but here if what he suspected was true.

He had thought that tonight would go so very differently. He'd believed that he would have to spend their first night as husband and wife persuading her into his bed. That he would need to take time and care with her, initiate her into lovemaking. He'd been prepared for that. He'd even anticipated a sort of extra pleasure in it as it awoke feelings, needs that had been buried in him too long. Now it seemed those needs had woken so fiercely that he was burning up inside just thinking of them. At the moment when he had to doubt, to fight, to recognise the dangers in what he was feeling.

And now, barely inside the room, he stopped and swung round to face Aziza.

'Come to me, my bride.'

My bride.

Aziza didn't know whether the shivers that ran down her spine at the sound of the words were the thrill of excitement or blind panic. The wedding night they were meant to share had been looming on the horizon like a heavy cloud, both terrifying and thrilling at the same time. She'd given her heart to this man all those years ago when she was still a child and had adored him from a distance ever since. But, following that meeting on the balcony on the night of the anniversary party, everything she had learned about him had challenged those fantasies.

Challenged but not destroyed them. They had soon pushed through her doubts, and this time they were blended in a dangerous, intoxicating cocktail with the new, adult, intensely female feelings she had for him. The feelings that a woman had for a man—and that she should have for the man who was her husband, who would father her child.

Just the thought of it took the strength from her legs so that she almost collapsed on to the floor. Hastily she covered it up by turning it into a curtsey instead, spreading out the rich golden robes of her wedding dress as she sank into a low sign of deference. It did not get the response she anticipated.

'No! Is this any way for a wife to greet her husband? On your feet, woman—and greet me as you promised.'

'As I—promised?'

'At the banqueting table—in return for the sweet treats I gave you.'

Now she understood. Part of it, at least. He wasn't just talking about the way she had used his name at his urging but the other, silent, sensual promises she had given him when she had taken the grape from him, moulding her mouth around his fingers.

'I thought you were angry. That I'd done something wrong.'

She was sure he'd been furious with her and that that had driven him to the unexpectedly hasty departure from his own wedding reception. But there was still something wrong with his tone, something that twisted deep inside her, warning her to tread carefully.

'Should I be angry?' Nabil demanded. 'Tell me— have you done anything wrong?'

'I thought that you thought perhaps I was too familiar...'

'You're the first person—apart from Clementina and Karim—the first person to behave in a real way ever since...'

He was thinking of Sharmila. Of the woman who had been his wife. His love. His life.

For a moment Aziza couldn't see straight enough to focus on the hand he held out to help her to her feet. Just in the same moment that he had given her something of what she yearned for, he had managed to take it all away again. In the heightened atmosphere of the ceremony, she had allowed herself to think that for once she was someone who mattered. Someone who was not just the 'other daughter', the one her father had to find a husband and provide a dowry for.

Now she knew that while she might be his bride, his

Queen, she was only a queen of convenience, chosen because his duty to the country demanded it. The wife of his heart was dead, and no one would ever replace her. Certainly not the woman he only remembered as a child all those years before. His 'other wife' as she now was.

'You treated me as a man.'

Nabil's voice had deepened, grown rough, and his hands tightened on her arms as he hauled her to her feet, holding her so firmly that she felt her skin must bruise where his fingers dug into her.

Why the hell had he had to remember Sharmila now, when those memories could only add to the brutal conflict inside him? It was those memories that stilled his hand, he realised, stopped him from grabbing at that damned veil and flinging it up over her head to see what she really looked like—who she really was. He should have done that immediately, revealed who she was from the start so that he knew what he was dealing with, but the simple fact that he had hesitated told him more than he wanted to know about his own feelings.

Damn it, he should have gone with his first instincts and taken the maid called Zia there and then on the balcony on the night of the celebration, when there would have been no legal, no dynastic, implications involved. If this was indeed Zia who had recognised his hunger for her and used it as part of a plot to trap him.

'A man you wanted. Was that true?'

'True?' Aziza echoed shakenly, the harsh demand in his tone making her see her own behaviour through his eyes, and quail inside at the thought of how brazen it must have seemed. 'Y-Yes.'

She had been so stunned by her own immediate and urgent response to him that she hadn't been able to hide it. He was a man whose reputation with women was

well-known. He had the freedom to play the field as he
wanted, but surely he was traditional enough to expect
a virgin, innocent bride? She was definitely the former;
any daughter brought up under her father's strict regime
would have to be untouched until married.

But what would Nabil want? How would he view her
after that admission? The whole reality of the moment in
her life she had come to ricocheted around her head. She
was married. To the most gorgeous, devastating male
she had ever met, and this was her wedding night. When
her husband would have the right to take her, to make
her his. Uncertainty flooded through her at the thought.
Was it possible that he was regretting his choice?

'And I want you.'

Nabil's voice, rough and raw, broke into her whirling
thoughts, setting her mind spinning off on to another
track altogether. Was it possible that she could have this
effect on this powerful, forceful male?

'But—everyone thought… Jamalia…'

'Your sister?' A brusque, almost violent gesture of
rejection underlined his words in a way that startled and
confused. 'Sure, she'd look wonderful on the stamps.
But you…'

The word sounded thick and raw, making a stunned
excitement start to uncoil in her stomach. The sting of
need that tightened her breasts was like an electric current passing through her so that she shifted uncomfortably where she stood.

'Damn it to hell, Aziza, but I hate this blasted veil.'

His fingers tangled in it, tugging at the delicate material roughly in a way that pulled painfully at the many
tiny pins that held it in place. 'How do we get rid of it?'

'Let me…'

The hand she put up to her head, hunting out the first

of the pins in her hair, shook almost as much as her voice. But at least she knew what she was doing with this. When her mother, aided by her personal maid, had put the veil on her, working her way around her head to fasten it to the twists and braids of the ornate hair style into which her black hair was piled up underneath, she had made sure that her daughter knew just where each fastening would be placed, and how many pins there were so that Aziza would know how to remove the concealing covering for herself.

'It's designed so that it won't move or come loose—until…'

Just for a second the flying fingers slowed, stilled, came to a complete stop with the last couple of pins in their reach as Aziza struggled with the reality of just what was happening. Apprehension fought with anticipation, a wild, fizzing excitement at the thought that this man—her husband—really had wanted her, not her sister.

'Done!' she managed on a long exhalation of breath, taking the veil in one hand, lifting it, flinging it in the opposite direction to the pins so that it rose wildly into the air, hovered for a moment then drifted slowly and elegantly down to the floor like some giant gauzy cloud.

Then she turned to see Nabil, to meet his eyes, for once free and unrestricted by the concealing curtains.

And saw his whole face change. Saw every muscle draw tight over his harsh, etched bone structure, pulling the skin white around the nose and mouth. Saw the light fade from his eyes to be replaced by a heavy shadow that spoke of the exact opposite of what she had hoped to see in his reaction.

He even took a single step backwards, away and so much more distant from her than the paces between them. His obvious mental withdrawal was far, far worse than any physical response he had made.

'Nabil…'

It was just a whisper, dragged from a mouth that was suddenly too dry to speak properly. Even as she said it, she was forced to wonder whether in fact that was the biggest mistake of all.

Had he given her permission to use his name? She'd thought he had, but as she met the polished jet darkness of those deep-set eyes she saw no lessening of the frozen coldness, no warming to soften them.

'Sire…' she tried again, anxious to repair the mistake—if a mistake it had been. Desperate to appease him she sank into a deep curtsey too, giving him the respect and deference he was owed as the Sheikh.

Her husband but still the Sheikh.

'Sire…' he muttered, echoing her shaken response with dark cynicism.

With a movement like the pounce of a hunting cat, he moved forward, reached for her left hand, grabbing it and lifting it from where it was partially hidden by the sweeping skirt of her wedding gown.

'Sire,' he said again and the danger in that dark tone drained all the power from Aziza's legs so that she could only stay crouched halfway to the floor, staring with unfocused eyes as she watched him lift the hand he'd captured, turn it so that he could see it more clearly. His black frowning gaze fixed on the slightly damaged shape of her littlest finger and too late she realised that he had stared at it in something of the same way before. On the night on the balcony.

The night when she had told him…

'Zia…' Nabil said again, his tone turning the sound

of her nickname into a fiendish curse. 'Not Aziza—but Zia.'

He spat the word at her, not troubling to hide the fury he was feeling.

'Hellfire and damnation—I have married the maid!'

CHAPTER SEVEN

HELLFIRE AND DAMNATION—I've married the maid!

Or have I?

Nabil tried to make his mind focus but nothing registered except the appalling truth of those seven impossible words. Was that his pulse thundering inside his head, beating at his temples, or had a storm really broken on the horizon, threatening to drown any attempt to think straight?

'Who the hell are you?'

No—stupid question. He knew exactly who she was—or did he? Aziza, his arranged bride—or Zia, 'just a maid'? Shaking his head violently as his scrambled brain refused to put any words together in a logical sequence, Nabil tried to enforce some control on the thinking processes that had been shattered by shock and savage rage. The fact that his body was still rock hard with desire only made matters even worse.

Just moments before he had been burning up with sexual hunger; turned on as he had never been before in his life. Now it felt as if someone had punched him right in the gut and the throbbing ache of frustration only soured his temper even more than the mental bruising.

'Who?'

He got a grim sort of satisfaction from the way she

started in nervous reaction as he flung the word into her white face. A face he'd been so impatient to see, never realising until too late that he'd seen it already, and so much more recently than the child Aziza he had been trying to remember.

Against the pallor of her skin, her golden eyes looked huge and dark, the lush fringes of her black lashes making them look even wider than before. He had been enchanted by those eyes that night on the balcony, he remembered. They had drawn him in like some witch's spell woven deliberately around him. Was it then that the plan to deceive him had come to her mind—or was there some other way that this scheme had been created? A *maid* couldn't have arranged all this by herself, could she? There had to be someone else behind all this. The answer seemed obvious.

How much had Farouk been planning all this time?

'Who put you up to this?'

'No one… I mean…'

For a moment it looked like she was about to get to her feet, then obviously thought the better of it. But the slight movement was enough to remind Nabil of the implications of the situation and to have him checking in the belt under his robe. Feeling the cool slide of metal there under his fingertips, he relaxed again and flung a repeat of the question at her with cold virulence.

'I asked you—*who*?'

'No one put me up to it.'

She'd regained some sort of strength in her voice and was able to make it sound as if she was actually defying him. He was glad to see that. He didn't want to see her go down without a real contest. He wanted a worthy opponent to give him a chance to release some of the tumult of emotions he was feeling inside.

All he should be feeling was anger and betrayal. He'd been deceived again, trapped—this wasn't Aziza, was it? But it was intensely disturbing to realise that there was so much more. The desire was only part of it.

'It was you.'

'Me! Are you mad, woman? Are you actually claiming that I...?'

Aziza—or Zia—or whatever her name was—had obviously had enough of being down on the floor. She put her hands to the floor and pushed herself upwards, scrambling to her feet as she faced him boldly, her neat little chin set into a firm declaration of defiance. Strangely, she looked even more defenceless standing before him like this when she had clearly tried to draw herself up to her full height.

'You are the one who asked me—who picked me out as his prospective bride.'

'Not you...'

He was remembering the moment when he had seen her and her mistress—Jamalia—through the two-way mirror, recalling the hot wave of physical hunger that had swept through him just from touching her, kissing her, on the balcony. The same hunger that had alerted him to the fact that something was not as he had anticipated when he had fed her the sugared grape at the banquet table.

When he had caught the scent of her perfume.

'I never chose *you*.'

Aziza winced under the sting of that lashing dismissal. She had been so overjoyed to think that Nabil had chosen her. That he wanted her above all the other candidates. The beautiful women he could have chosen. Even her sister. But he had picked her. The one her father had always believed was second best.

But now Nabil was saying that he hadn't chosen her—he didn't even want her! Her mind flashed back to the scene in the crowded, brilliantly lit banqueting hall. The knowing looks of the guests who had watched as Nabil had stood up and grabbed hold of her hand.

She had thought she knew what that meant. She'd believed that very soon she would be a proper wife, sharing her husband's bed. But now what would happen?

I never chose you.

How would she ever face everyone all over again and let them know that Sheikh Nabil—the man she had thought was to be her husband—had taken one look at her face and rejected her out of hand?

How could she go from being Queen one moment to a nobody—a rejected, spurned nobody—in less than a couple of hours? And how could she ever cope with knowing that Nabil had decided she was not the person he wanted? The thought of confronting her father's rage at her failure was as nothing when compared with the prospect of having to leave now, when it had seemed that so much—her dreams and fantasies—had been within her grasp.

Her body still thrummed from the sensual tension that had seared through it. Every nerve was stretched so tight she felt it would snap if she moved, and the stinging, burning need that his kiss, his touch, had woken so newly in her refused to subside while he was still so near, so close that she only had to reach out her hand...

It was only when she saw the way Nabil's head came up, the wary tensing of his long body, that she realised she had done just that, and somehow added fire to the suspicions he was already harbouring against her.

'You asked for Jamalia's sister,' she managed, stumbling over the words.

'And got her maid instead.' Could he put any more darkness, any further rejection, into the words? 'So what is this—some sort of plan to trap me, tie me into marriage with you?'

'Oh, no, no! Why would I want to trap you?'

Just the horror at the thought that he might actually believe she had wanted to do that propelled her forward jerkily, both hands coming out this time, reaching for him.

She never actually saw him move; never even registered the sudden blink that revealed his reaction, the swift, flash of action that intercepted and reversed their positions so that suddenly, instead of facing him, she had been grasped by the wrist and twisted round against him. Her back was tight up against the hard strength of his chest, her body imprisoned by the iron-hard bands of his arms.

And in his hand was the polished gleam of metal, the narrow shape of a wicked, sharply honed knife held so tight in Nabil's fist that his knuckles showed white where he gripped it hard.

'Nabil, no!'

Aziza tried to turn to face him, realising her mistake when his arms tightened round her even more and she could hear the thud of his heartbeat against her ear. It was that rapid and uneven pulse that told its own story, making her realise the truth. She should have thought; should have remembered. Now, too late, the recollection of the way he had started when a door had banged in the banqueting hall came back to haunt her with a new and disturbing significance. The terrible memory of the day that he had survived the assassination attempt flashed behind her eyes.

'You don't need that—really you don't.'

Immediately she made herself react, letting her body go limp against his as she held her own hands out in front of her, fingers splayed so that he could see there was nothing hidden there.

'I'm sorry—I'm not really Jamalia's maid—and there is nothing in this that was ever against you.'

At least she prayed not. Her father had seemed content enough with the marriage negotiations. He had never shown any inclination to turn his loyalties to the lingering group of revolutionaries who had threatened rebellion. But did Nabil suspect that he would?

'I would never harm you—I promise. We were friends once.'

Friends...

The word seemed to have so much more significance than he could ever have imagined, Nabil acknowledged. She had said that she was not Jamalia's maid and yet she was very definitely the woman he had met that night. If she truly was Aziza, his promised wife, the child who had been his friend now grown up, then he wanted to believe her—he wanted to trust her. But wanting to trust and being *able* to do so were two totally separate things, and the ability to think straight and read the signs accurately were severely compromised by the position he found himself in.

Her body was soft and lush against his, her waist where his arm was clamped around it impossibly narrow, and the curves of her hips and buttocks crushed up against his pelvis tormented his still aroused and hardened manhood. If she squirmed against him as she had done when he had first grabbed her then he would be lost. But instead it seemed that she had given up on any thought of action, her whole body loosening, almost sagging in his arms.

'I was friends with an Aziza once,' he said slowly. 'A long time ago.'

A lifetime. Everything that he had believed he had in that time had been taken from him and destroyed, shattering into tiny irreplaceable pieces. Had he hoped for something of that life to be returned to him when he had thought of Aziza, only to find that his choice had rebounded right into his face?

'And we never truly knew each other.'

With a sudden movement he spun her round in his arms so that she was facing him, golden eyes blazing straight into his. But it wasn't just defiance that he saw there. Instead it was something new, something infinitely disturbing. He had seen just such an expression in the eyes of a puppy when he had once kicked it accidentally on his way out the door. The elaborate makeup that adorned her face, even behind that blasted veil, had started to wear off, leaving her looking paler and strangely vulnerable. And the elaborate coils and braids of her hair had started to come loose in their struggle just moments before. She looked younger, gentler—more like the maid who'd had such a disturbing effect on him ever since that night on the balcony.

'Who the hell *are* you?' he growled, refusing to let himself admit to just what effect that spin of her body had had as it pressed her breasts and hips against him, making her perfume waft in the air. The slide of several silken strands of her hair against his face was almost the last straw as it caught on his mouth, on the dark hairs of his beard.

'I'm Aziza—I am!' she protested when she must have caught his sceptical frown. 'I'm both Aziza—and Zia. Yes, I'm that "maid" you met that night—really I am—but I was just trying to cover myself. I knew I shouldn't have been out there on my own—wandering about your palace without your approval. It's the truth!'

She looked innocent. Looked totally believable. And every masculine element in him wanted to believe her and get this over with. He had been anticipating a wedding night and he should be enjoying it now. The heated pulse in his body, the hardness between his legs, told him he would be enjoying it—if he could only let go of the black memories and suspicions that held his mind prisoner.

Sharmila had looked innocent too. He'd been caught that way before and he had no intention of letting it happen again.

'And why should I believe you?'

'Because I'm telling the truth. Because…'

Meeting the cynical question in his eyes, she let her voice fade away, dropped her gaze sharply, biting her lip as she did so. The impulse to lean forward, cover her mouth with his and lick away the sharp punishment she was inflicting on her soft skin was almost overwhelming. His own mouth actually watered for the taste of hers just as he'd shared it on the balcony. How had his world become turned inside out in so short a time?

'Because you have nothing to fear from me.'

Aziza's voice caught as she realised just what she was saying. What he had been saying with all this suspicion, the sudden cold distance. That terrible moment with the knife. In the back of her memory she saw again that moment when he had heard the door bang and had tensed sharply, almost imperceptibly, but she had caught it. How could she forget—how could anyone forget—that he had once been the victim of an assassination attempt?

'Nabil…'

He had let her use his name before, hadn't insisted

on the reverence due to him as the King, so she risked it again.

She shifted in his arms, still face to face with him. So close. She could even catch his breath in her nostrils and the crisp brush of his beard on her forehead.

'You can trust me—I promise. And, as to who I am, well, I am Aziza. Your chosen bride. My father's daughter.'

He was silent, still, watchful and alert. Those black eyes were polished jet, reflecting her own face back at her and giving nothing away.

'But I'm also Zia—the "maid" you met that night.'

Was his reaction one of acceptance or rejection? She only knew that the hands that held her had tightened and his head had gone back slightly.

'I was there with my family—with my father and Jamalia. I was supposed to be there to act as my sister's chaperone. But she didn't want me; I was cramping her style, and the party just wasn't my sort of thing. My head was pounding. I needed air.'

Gently she placed her hand on his arm, realising that it looked impossibly small against the swell of his muscles under the white robe. The slightly twisted little finger looked even more vulnerable like this. She watched his eyes drop to stare at it.

'It was very stuffy in there.'

Was that response any sort of a concession, or simply an acknowledgement of fact? At least he had spoken. That stony silence had stretched her nerves to snapping point.

'Your hand...'

It was low, rough. He shifted position slightly, lifted his own hand and traced the twisted line of the delicate bones, making her shiver in response.

'How did it happen?'

He'd been there when she'd been injured. But why would he remember?

'It was so long ago. Fifteen years, at least. When you were visiting us.'

'Fifteen years?' Nabil frowned as he took his thoughts back. 'You fell from your pony.'

He recalled the fuss when her small chestnut steed had reared in a panic at the sight of a snake and Aziza had tumbled from the saddle. They had been a long way out into the desert on that ride. It must have been a slow, painful journey back.

'Your sister *was* trying to keep my focus on her.'

Jamalia had been playing for his attention so much that day. Even back then, with his father still alive, before he'd actually become the Sheikh, it had been obvious that Farouk had hoped that his elder daughter would catch his eye. It had been the blatant attempts of Farouk to interest him in Jamalia that had put him off, Nabil recalled. As a result, he'd been an open target for a later, much more subtle approach. He hadn't seen Sharmila coming.

The flood of memories that thought brought made him scowl darkly and he watched the way his change of expression made her recoil against his arms.

'You were very brave.' That was what he remembered most. Her silence. Any other child would have cried; Aziza had clamped her mouth shut over whatever she'd been feeling.

'That's not what my father thought. He thought I was foolish—if I'd been a better rider then I'd never have fallen off. That's why he had me taken home—fast.'

He supposed, when he thought of it, that he remembered that too. At the time it had seemed that her father had focused on sending his younger daughter home to have her injury tended. Instead, he had been determined to make sure that nothing intruded on the time Jamalia spent with the Sheikh's son. But he remembered the poor, pinched little face of the injured child, and how she had put up with her injury without complaint. He'd been impressed at her courage and control. And he'd known a flash of anger at the way that her father had dismissed her distress, wanting to spend more time on the ride—more time bringing Jamalia to his attention.

'He forbade me to ride again after that, for fear that I would do more harm to myself and become damaged goods—even less valuable as a bride.'

It was no wonder he'd never liked or trusted Farouk El Afarim, Nabil thought grimly. But he hadn't realised that his memories went back that far.

Aziza had broken her finger and he had seen that same damage on Zia's hand the night they'd met. So this was Zia—but she also had to be Aziza too.

'It didn't mend too well.'

Once more his touch smoothed over the damaged bones, making Aziza shiver. *You were very brave.* So had he accepted her story, believing in what she told him? Certainly he recalled the young Aziza, and the day of her fall. But it hadn't done anything to reduce his tension. The long body against hers, the powerful arms that held her, were still taut with control.

'So that night—on the balcony. Why tell me you were the maid?'

When he thought of how much he'd wanted her. How close he'd come to seducing her. The drum of his pulse that seemed to have quietened now started up again, pounding at his temples, at the feel and scent of her, warning him not to trust too easily. Not to forget.

With an inward snarl he drove it away. All he wanted to do was to forget. But now here was this woman bringing back so many memories he thought he had buried. Hell, that first night he'd even thought she was Sharmila.

'Why call yourself Zia?' he asked sharply. 'Why not give me your real name?'

'And have my father know that I had been wandering about the palace unchaperoned? That I'd left Jamalia to her own devices?'

She gave a tiny shiver at the thought. And, recalling how her father had so obviously put her sister first, Nabil thought he could understand why.

'I gave that name because I knew I shouldn't be there.'

'So why "Zia"?'

The question changed something in her demeanour, made her expression close up, her eyes become shaded. She was hiding something there, he recognised. Each time it seemed that she had convinced him there was nothing shady behind her actions, she made a mistake, and that deep suspicion was back.

'Tell me!'

'It's just a shortening of my name. One the family uses.'

'And you expect me to believe all this?'

'It's the truth!' she protested. 'And you'd know it if you'd just listen.'

Her eyes lifted swiftly, golden gaze meeting his, and she gave an unexpected little smile straight into his watchful eyes.

'I want to convince you, sire. There must be a way I can do that.'

CHAPTER EIGHT

'LET ME CONVINCE YOU.'

It was half-plea, half-enticement.

Unexpectedly she lifted her arms—spread them out on either side of her, leaving her whole body open to him. The movement lifted those lush breasts high, putting temptation right there in front of him and forcing him into a brutal fight against his natural impulse to give in to that enticement without thinking.

'I know you believe that I could be planning to harm you, but I swear I'm not. So why don't you prove it—search me. Go on,' she urged when he didn't move. 'Check me out—you'll not find anything. I'm not carrying any weapon.'

Nothing except those wide, beseeching eyes, that rich, soft mouth, those glorious breasts... Did she know what it would do to him to touch her now when he was already so hot and hard in arousal just from having her against him?

She was Aziza—had to be Aziza—and so she brought with her everything he had looked for, everything he needed in this marriage. As Farouk's younger daughter, she ensured the benefits of the peace treaty, the alliance with her father, the future that this union offered for the country. Did he need to do this?

'Do it,' Aziza said sharply when he still hesitated, fighting a grim and brutal battle with himself against the urge to do just as she asked—more than she asked. To do what she was inviting.

But the truth was that it was what she was inviting that made him hesitate. Wasn't this the best way to distract him?

'I need to prove that I've not come here to harm you.'

If he was honest, Nabil acknowledged, then he would be all sorts of a fool to leave things just as they were. He needed to prove that she was harmless, that the pretence that she had been Zia the maid when really she was a member of the El Afarim family had been just an accident, not part of some other plot. But life had taught him that there were plots where you least expected them; and the most innocent, the most beautiful face could hide a lying, treacherous heart. It was the only safe, the only sensible thing to do. But he didn't feel at all safe and he didn't feel in the least bit *sensible* as he moved her slightly backwards, away from him, and, with the knife still held in one hand, carefully began to move the other hand across the glorious curves she offered him.

How the hell did security officers, his bodyguards, ever manage this? he asked himself as his fingertips patted over the silken robe, keeping to the safety of her neck and shoulders first, but then moving down, lower, over the slopes of her breasts, and underneath where the soft weight seemed to fall into his palms with wicked enticement.

He would have been all right then, too, if only he hadn't glanced up. Hadn't looked into her face and seen the way her eyes had darkened, their lids becoming heavy, hooded, as her breathing became deeper, slower too. He could feel her pulse, thick and heavy, and saw her head fall back, eyes closing slowly, her soft mouth opening slightly.

He was on very thin ice indeed. If he gave in too quickly to the hungry demands of his aroused body, he of all people knew how foolish that was. Hadn't Sharmila taught him anything? In the back of his mind he could hear her words—the words he had believed to be motivated by love and caring.

Come to bed, my lord, and make me your wife.

'Nabil…'

Aziza's whole body was burning up in response to his touch, her breasts tightening, heated moisture gathering between her legs. The feel of those hot, hard palms against her body, even with the fine silk of her wedding dress between them, was like being branded for life. Branded as his. Wherever he touched she thought that a trail of marked skin would follow the path of those tormenting fingers and she could barely stop herself from pressing into that scorching connection. When his searching hands swept down from below her tingling breasts to smooth over the curves of her hips, the intimate response that shuddered through her had her doing a small, uncontrolled little shimmy against his touch.

'As you see, I'm not hiding anything,' she managed, her throat raw and dry.

'No…' He sounded worse than she did.

'So take me to bed, my lord, make me your wife.'

Nabil's shocking response was a violently muttered curse. Unbelievably, he suddenly stopped his search, his hands frighteningly still for a moment.

'Enough,' he declared harshly, cold and withdrawn.

Enough? Aziza blinked hard, tried to stare at him through unfocused eyes. How could that be enough?

He must be as aroused as her. How could he switch it off, forget it in the space of a heartbeat?

But when she looked into his face it was as if it was dead, totally closed off and opaque. He had withdrawn into some secret space where she couldn't reach him and he snatched his hands away sharply, letting the heat evaporate and leaving her cold, jolting her out of the sensual dream she'd foolishly let herself drift into.

'I said *enough*!'

His hands came up between them, like a knife cutting off all connection; his face was so set and hard, each muscle taut.

'We are done.'

She was back to being Zia, the unwanted maid.

You stupid little fool—you wouldn't even know who you were kissing. What kind of man you wanted...

The words rang inside her head, harder now, more brutal than before and hitting home with cruel precision. Because this time she knew just who she had been kissing; and she very definitely knew what kind of man she wanted. She wanted Nabil and only him, her childhood crush flowering into a fully formed adult hunger. The trouble was that he couldn't have made it any plainer that she was not the kind of woman he wanted.

At least not in any way that he would admit to. But he had wanted her before—hadn't he? She had so little experience in these things so had she read it all wrong? Was it true that, as her father had always said, she was not the marriageable prospect that her sister was? Or had she shocked Nabil by appearing so forward, by displaying her need so openly?

'But now that you know I'm not concealing any weapon? That I'm no danger to you...?'

'Not unless *that* was your secret weapon,' Nabil flashed back, stunning her.

His searing look that slid over her bewildered face, lingering at her breasts and hips, confused her even further until she realised just what he was saying and her blood ran cold.

'You think that I was trying to seduce you into...'

'You were not trying—you were succeeding,' Nabil retorted but he managed to make it sound as if that was the greatest crime on earth.

She was forgetting that the man who had grabbed her hand and all but dragged her here from the banqueting hall had had his mind filled with thoughts of conspiracy and treachery. Did he really believe that she had set out to seduce him, to distract his thoughts from the realisation he had been deceived...betrayed? The memory of the moment he had pulled out the knife made it feel as if the weapon had twisted in her own heart.

She had tried so hard to make him believe that she was someone he could trust, even submitting to that brutally intimate search, letting his hard fingers go wherever they wanted on her body. She could still feel the scorch they had left behind.

'As I said, we are done.' The ultimate dismissal.

Just for a moment Aziza almost returned to the mood of the night when they'd met on the balcony. When she had been pretending to be Zia the maid. He had spoken in the same dismissive way then, wanting rid of her as quickly as possible. Once again she'd been ordered to leave the presence of the Sheikh, dismissed by him, and this time her response was very nearly the same. She even let her hands drop to gather the golden folds of her skirt, ready to dip into the respectful curtsey protocol demanded. But then she met Nabil's cold-eyed stare once more and knew a welcome rush of rebellion.

No. The word reverberated inside her head so strongly that she felt sure Nabil must hear it too. But the brutal glare showed no response, no alteration in his expression. She felt the change in herself, though, and was determined to act on it. He had chosen her once even if the dark suspicions built by something in his past had caused him to go back on that decision. She would show him that, even if he didn't believe it as yet, she had his best interests and that of the kingdom at heart.

'So you want me to go out there…'

With a wave of her hand she gestured towards the closed door through which he had bundled her such a short time before.

'And let everyone see that this marriage has failed already? To tell my father that the treaty is null and void—dead in the water?'

And that her father was correct when he'd said that his 'other daughter' was not a suitable wife for the Sheikh.

'As you wish.' She made her voice as cold as his had been.

Then she drew herself up, lifted her chin and turned on her heel. Not even glancing back over her shoulder to see his response, refusing to let it look as if she cared, she took one step away from him, then another.

'One moment.'

It came from behind her, brutal and hard as a bullet hitting her between her shoulder blades.

'Where the hell do you think you're going?'

Was he going to let her go? Nabil demanded of himself. Was he actually going to let her walk out of here and take with her everything that this whole marriage arrangement had been about? Was he really going to throw away the peace and prosperity of the country, the heir that his throne needed so badly?

'I believe that you said we are done. If that is the case then I don't intend to wait around for you to decide whether you trust me or not.'

It wasn't her he didn't trust, but her father. Farouk had been scheming for this wedding for so long that he could believe Aziza's father would do anything to make it work. Even accept that the daughter Nabil had chosen had not been the one he had wanted him to marry. It was strange but now, when she was walking away from him, his mind was filled with the most vivid image of when they had first met, when she had fallen from that pony and broken her finger. She must have been in pain and distress, but her small back had been straight, her head held high as her nursemaid had hurried her away. She was so much taller now, her figure that of a woman, not a child. But it wasn't the physical change that struck him. It was the proud defiance, the *regal* elegance of her figure.

He had spent too long thinking of the gentle child Aziza had been that it was a shock to realise she had become a woman—all woman. Even more of a shock to recognise that she was the woman he had lusted over when she had told him her name was Zia. If he let her go now then he was losing more than just the treaty and doing his duty by the country. This wasn't for Rhastaan, this was personal.

But in that case, trust was all the more important. He'd rushed into this marriage with too little thought. He'd weighed the pros and cons of the arranged marriage with a cool head, but he'd chosen Aziza in a very different mood. The last time he'd done that it had ended with marriage to Sharmila, and the fallout from that had scarred so much more than his face. If there was one thing that experience had taught him, it was to be wary, that nothing was what it appeared on the surface.

He had time to spare on this. He could bank the treaty, play a careful game, and see if he might get more out of it than he had ever planned. One thing he was sure of was that he was damned well not going to lose the women who had sexually excited him most in years if he could help it.

'Did I give you permission to leave?'

'Do I need your permission?'

She wanted to resist—wished she had the strength to tell him to go to hell and turn and walk away. But she knew she wasn't going to manage that. How could she try for any other reaction when she'd already given him the message he wanted simply by staying at all?

She had to prove to him that she could be trusted. That there was no conspiracy at all behind her appearance as his potential bride. What else could she do? If Nabil suspected her father, her whole family would be in danger, her mother and sister disgraced.

The memory of the moment he had taken her from the banqueting hall, the way that her father had had to bow as she passed, the look on Jamalia's face when Farouk had said those words *he has chosen you*, all combined to put a touch of steel in her spine, fire up her blood. She could see his face reflected in a mirror on the wall, the dark scowl that brought his black brows together.

'I am the King,' he growled now.

'And I am your Queen. Well, that's true, isn't it? Or was our marriage illegal in some way?'

She waited a nicely calculated moment, watched his face freeze, those black eyes flashing dangerously.

'You wanted to know who I am—well, I'm not Zia the maid, or even just Aziza any more. I am the Sheikha, the Sheikh's chosen wife, by marriage at least if not in actual fact.'

That hit home. She saw his eyes go to the bedroom door, then back again, fixing on her so strongly that she felt the force of his stare like a laser burn at the back of her head.

'You took me as your wife today and as such I no longer need to bow down to anyone.'

His smile was deadly. A quick, rough quirk of his lips that warned of something dangerous to come.

'Outside this room, perhaps. But surely you know that a marriage needs to be consummated before it becomes formally finalised—a fact rather than just a declaration of intent?'

'Consummated...'

This time she couldn't help herself. She turned partway, then froze again as she met the black ice of his stare. Just hours before, her foolish young heart had dreamed of sharing this man's bed, of giving him her body, because he had made her feel special, chosen— *wanted*. It had been the fulfilment of her adolescent dreams. But that was when she'd believed he wanted her more than any other woman.

Now she dreaded the possibility because she knew that he saw her only as his to command. A pawn in the treaty negotiations. He didn't even trust her and her attempts to explain had been dashed aside.

Did he really expect her to stay, to share his bed tonight? Of course he did. That was what this marriage had always been about. But that was before he had believed that she and her family had somehow deceived him.

Then there was that other vital reason he had married her. He needed an heir, so did that override his dark distrust?

'Are you saying that you believe me now? That you don't think that I married you under false pretences? So do I go or do I stay?'

Her thoughts dried up as Nabil prowled towards her, silent-footed, as sleek and dangerous as a beautiful black panther stalking his prey.

Coming level with her, he slid his hand under her chin to lift her face when she tried just to stare at the ground to avoid him.

'You stay.'

His smile was deadly, steely-eyed, with a twist to his mouth that had nothing of warmth in it. It was a smile that spoke of possession, of ownership. The smile of a man who knew he was the ultimate ruler; that he held her fate in the palm of his hand.

'Walk out that door and you take with you your own reputation and that of your family. As you are so determined to point out to me, you are now my Queen and as such you are expected to share my room. My bed.'

His cold-eyed gaze left her face and drifted over towards the door into his bedroom. If there was anything that brought home to her just how much things had changed since the moment they had almost stumbled through that door in a hot-blooded rush, she'd thought for the bed, it was the look that was stamped on to his stunning features. Every muscle in his face was set hard as stone, his jaw tight, those sensual lips clamped into a thin, hard line.

Did that twist of her heart, the sudden fluttering in her throat speak of excitement or fear? Was she always condemned to suffer ambiguous feelings about this man? At one moment wishing to be anywhere but here, at another knowing that she would be the target of bitter disappointment if she was never to know him fully.

'Oh, you need not look so appalled, *habibti*.'

He actually smiled when he saw her expression.

'I think that neither of us wants to rush into anything tonight. The country needs an heir but for tonight the country must wait. It has waited years already—what will one more night matter?'

He couldn't let her go, Nabil acknowledged inwardly. He had known that as soon as he had seen her turn and walk towards the door. But he knew only too well where his reckless desire for another woman had led him. Once the ghost of Sharmila had come between them, everything had been blackened and distorted by those memories.

Aziza or Zia were one and the same it seemed, but he still had to question whether that meeting on the balcony had been as innocent as it had appeared or something else. He knew what he wanted to think, but what he wanted had only shown him in the past that where women were concerned he was a fool, and a blind one at that.

As a king, he needed a queen. As a man, he needed a woman. When he had seen Aziza walk away from him, her head held high, her back as straight as a spear, those lush hips undulating with every step she took, she had looked every inch a queen: beautiful, stately, regal. And he had wanted her like the devil.

He still wanted her. So much that his whole body hurt. Even as he had come out with that 'one more night' line, his unappeased desire had been like a scream in his head.

She was his *wife* for goodness' sake! What he wanted

to do was to grab hold of her, lift her from her feet and carry her into the bedroom—throw her down on to the black silk covers and lose himself in the heat and beauty of her body.

Hell, no! There was more to play for here than just a night of hot sex. This marriage was supposed to have been for the future of the country. He was not prepared to take risks with it.

'We have all the time in the world. So you can have my bed tonight—without me in it. I will take the couch.'

'Oh, but...'

The protest tumbled from those plump rose-tinted lips as her eyes widened in shock—distress at being caught out? Or was she really as concerned as she appeared?

'Surely the couch will be too small—uncomfortable for you? I should sleep there.'

'Still playing the dedicated maid, little one?' he murmured, smiling down into her uplifted face. But it was a smile that chilled the evening air, her stomach twisting into tight, painful knots. 'I'm flattered—but there is no need for your concern. Believe me, in the desert I have slept on far harder beds, or no mattress at all. I will be fine.'

If he slept at all. The thought of lying through the long hours of the night knowing that Aziza was only metres away amongst the soft cushions of his bed left him doubting that he would enjoy a moment's sleep throughout the night.

'And I suppose you still want to make sure that I don't try to sneak out in the night, to meet with the fellow conspirators you have imagined I'm working with?'

Aziza's head came up, golden eyes blazing defiance above pale cheeks that had been drawn tight across her fine cheekbones. The Queen was back and it twisted in his guts to see her there, cursing the need for caution that held him back from enjoying the wedding night he had anticipated.

'It must be hell to be so cynical about people—and always looking for something underneath the surface, never trusting anyone.'

'You get used to it.'

The admission shocked Aziza, stunning her into silence. Once again her thoughts were torn in two different ways, feeling both repelled at the black cynicism of his statement and troubled at the thought of what had made him live like this. When his hand went up to rub at the scar on his cheek, she was tormented by images of the day he had been injured, the way he still reacted to any possible threat.

In spite of herself her hand went up, wanting to touch his face, ease the discomfort of that wound—in all ways. But the look in his eyes, the way his head jerked backwards, stopped the movement as it began.

'You can trust me.'

'I will decide when—if—that is true. For now, this is how it is to be.'

Without warning he took one step forward and, bending his head, brought his lips down hard on hers, crushing her mouth open so that the intimate taste of him flooded her senses, weakened her knees. Just a couple of heartbeats and then it was over. He was retreating from her, pushing her towards the bedroom as he swung away to the huge windows that looked down into the courtyard where the wedding festivities were still going on, the celebrations mocking the reality of the way the promised wedding night had turned out for the bride and groom.

'Go to bed, wife,' he commanded harshly. 'I will see you in the morning.'

Deliberately he turned his back on her, folding his arms across his broad chest as he stared out at the darkened city below. He obviously didn't spare her a single further thought but, as Aziza stumbled wearily in the direction of the bedroom she had expected to share with her groom that night, that kiss left her knowing that even without trust, without any form of affection, one touch, one caress, could still set molten desire pouring through her veins in a way that left her hungering for more.

CHAPTER NINE

Six days had passed since the wedding day.

Six nights since the wedding night that wasn't.

Six days of being a bride but not a wife.

Six days of being Queen to everyone in the country—but not to the one man who mattered. She'd even had to be at his side during the planned six days of celebrations that marked the royal wedding. Dressed as a queen, treated as a queen, knowing that as soon as they returned to their suite she would once more, like Cinderella, turn back into the insignificant maid she had once claimed to be. Never being anything to Nabil but a source of suspicion. Never knowing if he was going to renounce her and hand her back to her father in disgrace.

And what made matters worse was that each evening they'd been escorted to the royal suite of rooms with smiles and choruses of delight and left there, obviously meant to turn their attention to the vital matter of creating that all-important heir to the throne. Instead of which they had spent so much of their time in awkward silence until it had come time to prepare for bed.

Six nights of being in his bed—but without him. Six nights of not sleeping at all, but tossing and turning restlessly in spite of the luxury of her surroundings. And if she had fallen asleep at all then the restless, wildly erotic nature of her dreams piled sensation on sensation, making her heart race. She didn't know how many times she had lived through that terribly intimate search in her dreams. She only knew that in the darkness of her night-time imagination it felt even more heated, even more sensual than anything she had ever experienced in her life.

Waking had only brought coldness and shock, leaving her shivering in frustration, lost and bereft, unable to control her racing thoughts.

Six nights of that and she felt like a wreck, worn out from lack of sleep and from living each day on her nerves.

Today they had been to the farewell banquet for all their guests. She had spent a long time sitting beside Nabil on the ornate throne to which he had led her after their marriage, a throne she felt she had no real right to. As a result she had been unable to eat anything more than a mouthful or two while the ceremonial event had passed in a haze. Then she had spent more than an hour standing at Nabil's side as they'd said farewell to their guests. This at least had given her something to do; her studies came into use and she was able to greet so many of the dignitaries in their own language.

At last all the formal events were over and once more she was free to return to their suite where she sank down wearily into a chair and kicked off her elegant shoes.

'You did well today.'

The voice from the door surprised her and she glanced up, startled. She had been so sure that today, with the official ceremonies complete, Nabil would be free to find his own space, and that he would decide to leave her alone, give himself the privacy neither of them had had over the past week.

'I—thank you.'

Was he as tired as she was? As tired of the ceremonies and ritual, at least. His voice sounded flat enough for it, though he showed no sign of the sheer bone-aching fatigue that she had endured for the past couple of days. Nights with little sleep, the nerve-stretching tension of not being trusted, and every minute of the ceremony that she had no experience of would do that. For the past few nights she had pretended exhaustion as an excuse to crawl into the sanctuary of the bedroom and hide away. Tonight she took refuge in the same excuse.

'I'll leave you in peace…'

She was pushing herself to her feet when Nabil shook his head abruptly.

'Stay where you are. I've brought this for you.'

Aziza stared in disbelief at the plate of food he held out to her. Small, tasty-looking delicacies and some fresh fruit. Nothing complicated, nothing fancy. But what mattered more was that he had thought to provide it—and that he was now delivering the snack to her in person, not at the hands of one of the hundreds of servants who lived only to perform such tasks for him.

'Thank you.' Her throat had closed up so tight that it was an effort to push the words from it, and when she had to take the fine china plate from him her hand shook so badly that she almost dropped it down on to her knees.

'I noticed that you barely ate a crumb at the banquet. And, as you've disappeared into the bedroom every night before this, I thought I'd better make sure you eat before you did that. And I know I need this.'

He set down a jug of fresh mango juice on the table, adding two glasses and pouring some of the liquid into each of them. Aziza could only watch in silence as he tossed his headdress aside, shrugging off his outer robe, then gulped down a draft of the drink, the muscles under the tanned skin of his strong neck tightening with each swallow, before he dropped into a chair opposite her.

'Eat,' he commanded but there was an unexpected gentleness in his tone, not the autocratic snap she was used to.

The mango juice was needed first, her mouth too dry to eat anything. But once the glorious refreshment had been swallowed she found she really was ravenously hungry and the delicate pastries were a delight that practically melted on her tongue.

'This is wonderful,' she managed, but the quick glance up towards his face was a mistake, so that she dropped her gaze to her food again rather than let his laser sharp focus on her destroy the appetite she had just rediscovered. 'And thank you for saying that I did well—I wanted to do my best.'

'More than your best' was the unexpected response, almost making her choke on a crumb of pastry. 'I never knew you could speak so many languages.'

'Oh, that.' A small, slightly rueful bubble of laughter escaped her. 'To be honest I didn't do so very much except thank them in their own language, and at the very least wish them a safe journey home.'

'They appreciated it—and so did I.'

'Really?' She risked a swift upward glance through her lashes, stunned to see that his steady regard was calm, almost thoughtful.

'Why so surprised? Surely you can understand that

everyone appreciates the courtesy of being spoken to in their own language?'

'I was glad of a chance to try out my knowledge. I always loved studying languages. I begged my father to let me have extra lessons so that I could learn. He dismissed the idea of my going to university but he let me have conversational classes at home.'

That frown told her what he thought of her father's decision.

'Why not university? Did he think I brought in the new laws that meant women could attend universities— study for a degree—simply to have that ignored?'

'He believed that I would be even harder to find a husband for if it was known that I was bookish.'

'Your father is a fool.'

The bluntness of his retort made her blink in shock. Having endured so much mockery as she'd stumbled through her language lessons, her father's frank disbelief that she would master one other tongue, let alone the three she could now manage, it brought a glow of pride to her heart to know that this at least had been appreciated.

'He should be proud of you. I was proud of you tonight. And yesterday.'

'You were?'

Aziza dropped the pastry she had picked up back down on to the plate uneaten. Her throat suddenly felt thick and clogged and she had no wish to choke on her food.

Nabil's eyes met her shocked ones, still calm, but so intent that she felt they might burn deep into her soul.

'I would have told you that last night but you vanished into your room so fast and, by the time I looked in on you, you were fast asleep.'

'You looked in on me?'

It was a disturbing thought that he had caught her asleep and so vulnerable. She could only pray that nothing of her dreams, those wild desolate dreams into which she had tumbled when tiredness had finally ended her uneasy restlessness, had shown on her face.

'I wanted to talk to you. And the maid needed your dress to clean.'

'Oh, but I would have done that…'

Aziza's protest died away as she saw the glance he slanted her. A mixture of reproof and disbelief. Fiery colour rushed into her face as she recalled just why her dress had needed cleaning. They had visited a children's hospital and she hadn't been able to resist getting close to the young patients.

'I do know how to do it.'

'And so does the maid. It's her job.'

'And mine is to be—what?' When he didn't answer, she tried another approach, hoping to get him to answer her. 'I don't know how to be a queen.'

And there she'd touched on the reason he had wanted to talk to her last night, Nabil acknowledged.

'There was no one who could have done things any better.'

She'd had a natural, easy approach with everyone she met. The people she'd talked to had positively glowed in the warmth of her attention. And the children in the hospital they'd visited yesterday had made straight for her like needles drawn to a magnet. They had climbed all over her, pushed their hands into hers. Her elegant blue dress had come back smeared with sticky little fingerprints and a smattering of baby sick on one shoulder.

And she'd *laughed* at it! Laughed and gone back for more.

'I saw you before each event; you were nervous…'

'Terrified,' Aziza slipped in jerkily. 'I was never trained to be a potential queen—or married to anyone important. Not like Jamalia. So I tried to imagine what your mother would do—she was so elegant…'

Nabil hastily caught back the cynical laugh that almost escaped him. But he'd obviously not been quick enough to hide his response as it drew Aziza's eyes, wide with shock, to his face.

'You obviously didn't know my mother. She expected to be given attention—not to give it to others. And she would have hated to have children mess up her clothes. She would have made sure to keep a careful distance.'

'But surely with you—with her son?'

This time he wasn't so successful at hiding his cynicism.

'As I said, you didn't know my mother. Oh, she had style, elegance—*she* definitely looked good on the stamps. The person who most reminds me of her is your sister.'

'And that's not a good thing?'

Her eyes were like molten gold, fixed on his face. He couldn't look away.

'My mother wanted to be Queen much more than she ever wanted to be a mother. Once I arrived, she'd done her duty to the crown. One heir to the throne—check! Mission accomplished. With me safely under the care of my nurse she could go back to enjoying being the foremost lady in the land.'

'Enjoying it?' Aziza gave a small shudder. 'Is it possible to enjoy being the focus of every eye? Knowing that people are watching your every move?'

She looked so horrified that he wanted to wipe that distress from her face. If she had felt so disturbed by the past few days then she hadn't shown it when they were in public. After just a few short minutes he had known that he could leave her to cope, to talk to people whatever their age or status, though he had been aware of the way that every now and then she had glanced at him for support, encouragement.

'It's possible to grow accustomed to it at least. Believe me, Zia, it won't always be this bad.'

'Don't call me that!' Aziza couldn't hold back. She hated hearing that version of her name on his lips.

'Don't call you—what?' A dark frown pulled his black brows together. 'Zia?'

The sudden inclination of his head showed how he had caught the small flinch that was her reaction.

'It's how you introduced yourself to me.'

'When I didn't want you to know who I was.'

He was too aware, too sharp. She knew that when she saw his eyes narrow swiftly. And his response only confirmed it.

'So you don't want me to know Zia—but who is *Aziza*? Your father's daughter.'

'My father's second daughter.'

She'd intrigued him now. She saw the change in his expression, the tightening of the bronzed skin over the high, fierce cheekbones, then suddenly he was leaning forward with his arms resting along his thighs, hands clasped on his knees.

'Go on. Aziza, I said, go on,' he repeated when she hesitated and the note of command that came so naturally to him left her in no doubt that if she did not obey then the consequences would not be pretty.

'I— Well you know the "heir and a spare" syndrome? When there is the heir apparent—but a second son will be useful just to make sure? So a second son is only there in case they're needed—as back-up—well, the spare.'

'I understand.' It was clipped and curt. 'There have been times I might have wished that I'd had a brother—as "back-up" or at least as company—but how does this affect you?'

'That "spare" situation—well it works for daughters too. Perhaps even more so. My father always wanted a son—he didn't get one. He had two daughters—the first-born was special. She might not be a son and heir but she was a beauty who could be married off for a great bride price—bring honour to the family. And Jamalia was exactly that. She's always had suitors flocking to her. Not me. I was a second daughter—a disappointment.'

'How could anyone see you as a disappointment?' Nabil asked softly.

It could have meant so much. Perhaps on their wedding night it would have made all her dreams come true. But there had been that wedding night and that appalling moment when he had first seen her.

'You did. *"Hellfire and damnation—I've married the maid!"*,' she quoted hotly when she saw him frown in confusion. The stab of distress at his obvious disappointment was just as brutal—worse—than the first time she had heard it. 'And you looked so—horrified.'

He had said that he wasn't disappointed, but how could he have been anything else? He had thought that he was gaining a queen, instead...

'I suspected there might be a trap. I've been caught that way before.'

Aziza wasn't quite sure exactly how his face had changed. There was a new and disturbing tension that stretched his skin tight over his carved bone structure and a muscle jerked at the edge of his jaw where it was clamped tight against some feeling he was not prepared to admit.

'There are conspiracies everywhere.'

Could his eyes get any colder, bleaker? And without seeming to be aware of it he had lifted a hand to rub at the place where the scar marked his skin, just for a moment before he snatched his fingers away and shook his head in brusque rejection of his troublesome thoughts.

'And you thought I might be part of one.' She didn't know if the sadness in her voice was for herself and his suspicions of her or for the man who had grown up facing a rebellion against his rule that had been part of his father's legacy to him, and had obviously never fully recovered from that brutal attempt on his life and its fatal consequences.

No wonder he had been so determined not to let her close. She felt the cold slide of ice down her spine as she recalled the way that he had pulled the knife—a knife he obviously always had hidden about his person. And of course, every day he looked in the mirror, that scar must remind him that someone had hated him so much that they had tried to take his life. Something caught and twisted cruelly in her heart at the thought of him living with the fear and the doubt.

'Not me,' she hastened to assure him.

To her astonishment he didn't argue. Instead he seemed to accept her assurance, nodding slowly.

'You were not what I expected. But that was not disappointment. I wanted you in my bed from the moment I saw you. If you want to know the truth, it was the thought that you were Jamalia's maid that meant I had to think again about having her as my Queen.'

'You were watching us?'

She'd felt that he was there; had sensed the burn of

somebody's gaze coming through the two-way glass—observing them, watching every single move.

'Do you think I'd have chosen your sister, sight unseen?'

It was when he had seen the sensually feminine form of the woman he'd thought was just Zia that he had known he could not take Jamalia into his bed. Nor was she what he wanted as the mother of his children. He'd been there himself, and still remembered the loneliness, the shadowed world of being the wanted heir but not a wanted child. What was it Aziza had said? The first born could be married off—bring honour to the family. So had she too known what it was like to be a child who was wanted only to be there because of what they were worth in political terms?

'Seeing that maid reminded me of Jamalia's sister—of you. Had I but known it…'

And yesterday he'd had the evidence that his thoughts had been on the right track. The woman who hadn't cared about her clothes, who had let the children swarm all over her and had laughed, was the woman he wanted as mother to his children.

With Sharmila it had seemed as if it was like that too. She had appeared to want a child so much—more than he had at the time. It was almost as if she had set herself to get pregnant as quickly as possible. She *had* set out to do that, he acknowledged bitterly. If they weren't involved in the ceremony of court then they were in bed. It had suited him at the time, but that was before he had learned what was behind her apparent passion. The fact that she needed to cover up the betrayal she had already committed.

One thing Sharmila would never have done was kick off her shoes and curl up on a sofa as Aziza was doing now. They had never been able to share the quiet evenings when all the business of the court was done and they could just be the two of them. A man and a woman.

A sudden thought struck him, had him pausing and frowning. With a shock he realised that he had probably shared more with Aziza tonight than he had ever talked about to Sharmila. He had certainly never discussed his mother with his first wife.

'Aziza…' he began but as he looked at her he caught the way her hand flashed up to hide the yawn she was unable to hold back. Her eyelids were drooping heavily and she was practically dropping in her seat.

'You're exhausted,' he said and saw his pronouncement confirmed even as she tried to deny it by straightening in her chair, forcing herself to stay awake to continue their conversation. The half-eaten plate of food was in danger of sliding off her knee and it was only by making a grab for it that he stopped it from tumbling to the floor.

'Go to bed.'

The struggle he was having to hold on to his determination not to take a reckless step into a situation where he still wasn't sure of his facts made it sound more like a command than he had intended. Tired as she was, he saw the way she fought to lift her head enough to glare at him in defiance, though those beautiful eyes were cloudy with fatigue. Something twisted deep inside him and in spite of himself a small laugh escaped.

'You really need some sleep, Aziza,' he said, holding out a hand to help her to her feet.

She hesitated, then put her hand into his, letting him pull her from the chair. When she swayed where she stood, he almost lifted her off her feet to carry her to the bedroom. Hell but he wanted to do that. But the touch of her hand on his, warm skin on skin, and the wave of perfume mixed with her own personal scent, was temptation enough and he knew that if he did then it wouldn't stop there. He'd acted on these instincts before; he'd believed in Sharmila, had had his trust totally shattered. The report he had ordered would not be presented in its final form until tomorrow. Surely he could wait twenty-four hours for total peace of mind? Besides, Aziza was clearly so worn out it would be cruel not to let her sleep tonight.

But his hand felt empty, his spirit too, as she took her fingers from his and stumbled towards the bedroom, swaying with tiredness. It was only when the door swung to behind her, slotting into its frame with a bang, that he remembered earlier that night, when they had been busy with the farewells to their guests, that a car had backfired sharply close nearby. He had barely felt the old tension twist in his nerves before he had sensed Aziza's fingers, small, soft and gentle, slide into his and hold them reassuringly. Just for a moment. Just long enough for her to feel that he had relaxed, and then she had eased her hand away and turned her attention back to the conversation she'd been having with the French ambassador's wife.

He could wait twenty-four hours, but no more. That report had better say everything he needed it to say. The thought of anything else was the stuff of nightmares.

CHAPTER TEN

'Why are we here?' Aziza demanded as soon as it was safe to speak openly.

The day hadn't gone anything like the way she had expected. She had woken to find that the maid Nabil had assigned to look after her was in her dressing room, putting clothes into a case.

'Madam, His Highness says that I am to pack for you.'

'Why, where are we going?'

'To the mountain palace,' another voice had joined in. A male voice, deep and vibrant.

Nabil…

'But why?'

He hadn't answered her then, nor had he offered a word of explanation during the journey here. Having gone to bed with the hope that they had at least made some sort of progress from the way that they had talked the previous night, Aziza found this silence oppressive and disturbing. But, short of making a fuss in front of their driver, she had recognised that it was far better to remain silent until they actually arrived, and so had had to sit stiffly beside her supposed-to-be husband, hiding everything she felt from him.

But now at last they had reached the smaller, less

formal mountain palace and she was left alone with him in the royal apartments.

'Why have you brought me here?' she demanded again when Nabil did not speak.

Nabil turned a dark, sidelong glance on her.

'So that we can begin again.'

That caught her on the raw because she didn't know how to take it.

'Don't you think that "begin" is actually the correct term? After all, nothing really started between us—did it? So why have you decided that we can begin something now? What about all your suspicions—your belief that I was involved in some sort of plot against you?'

'I had you checked out.'

Nabil showed no hint of any feeling and his statement was so matter-of-fact it was almost totally blank.

'So I presume I passed the test, then?'

'If that is how you want to see it.'

'What other way is there to see it? I didn't know that there was to be an examination into how to be a queen, or that I'd have to wait until you decided that I was worthy of your attentions. After all *you* picked me. Didn't you?'

'I did.' If it was a concession, it didn't sound like one.

'Oh, that's good—because I thought that you had a check list that you handed out to your ministers.'

Something in his face attracted her attention, had her frowning as she looked deep into his eyes.

'You did, didn't you? Well that's a pretty cold-blooded way of going about things.'

'It was a *rational* way of going about things. After all, this is an arranged marriage—I understood that you knew what was expected of you. Would it help if I said that you passed every test with flying colours?'

'Is that supposed to be a compliment?'

'What do you think I was saying to you last night?' Nabil countered. 'Or were you too tired to take it in?'

Last night's memories were hazy at best, the fog of exhaustion blurring them. But he had brought her food, had told her she had handled the ceremonials well. He had even shared the truth about his mother with her and so she had gone to bed feeling better than she had for days. But she had still gone to bed alone.

'It wasn't just you that I had to have investigated. I needed to know exactly what your father had planned.'

'Oh, you needn't have worried about that.' Aziza refused to let that concession mean anything to her. 'If he'd wanted to plan anything underhand, it wouldn't have been me he'd have used. He'd never have expected that you'd choose me, for one, and he'd never believe I'd be capable of carrying it off. And, if you want to be sure that you can rely on him now, then the fact that you took his second daughter off his hands will probably ensure that.'

'The spare…' Nabil murmured, stunning her with the realisation that he really had been listening the night before. He was watching her, sharp, clear eyes, following every movement, every expression. It was as if he was waiting for something but she had no idea what.

'I assume that you had my sister checked out too—but you didn't choose her. So what made the difference?'

'I would have thought that was obvious.'

'Not to me.'

Nabil crooked a long finger, beckoning her. And this time his sensual mouth had softened into something close to a curve.

'Come here and I'll show you.'

She was almost trapped by his smile. But the memories of the wedding night were still too clear, too raw.

She had no wish to fall into that trap again. To try to reach out and grasp some wonderful little thread of hope, only to have it snatched away from her, leaving her lost and empty as before. She'd been cleared by his investigators, so now she was expected to fall into his hands like a ripe little plum. The fact that she yearned to do exactly that only made her own inner turmoil so much worse.

'I don't want to,' she tried now, determined not to give him the easy victory she knew he was expecting.

That curve grew, became a knowing smile.

'And you, my lovely wife, are a liar. A very bad one.'

It was dangerously soft, almost gentle, but all the same it sent a shiver down her spine.

'Will it help if I tell you how I feel? If I let you know the truth of what these past six days have done to me?'

He shouldn't have reminded her of the six days since their wedding. Nabil might think he had her in his power by force of strength and control. If only he knew that she was there because of something much stronger, much more unbreakable.

Wasn't the truth that she had stayed because she couldn't bear to go? Because, in spite of everything, she still foolishly, impossibly, held on to those dreams she had had of him when she was young? There had been tiny moments when the hard, set mask he wore day in and day out had seemed to slip and there was a glimpse of someone else underneath. Someone she wanted to know more about.

She had wanted to stay to try to reach *that* Nabil. To reach him and show him that whatever had made him so cynical so young was not inevitable and unchangeable. She had wanted him to know that there was someone he could trust. But also, digging deep down and star-

ing the truth right in the face, hadn't she also wanted
to stay because she *couldn't* leave him?

She was here because she still loved him, never having lost that heartfelt crush she had held for him all
those years ago; she had never grown out of it as she
matured. And now, as a woman, she felt the same. But
this time it was deepened and complicated by the rec-
ognition of the primitive call of his male body to hers,
the power of sexual hunger that no one else had ever
awoken in her.

And Nabil knew that. She didn't have to say a word. It
was there in every look she gave him, the way her eyes
lingered on his body, the irresistible draw of his mouth,
so that she felt her own lips tingle whenever she saw it,
remembering the way he had tasted. And it was there
in the way she tossed and turned at night, restless even
on the silken sheets, waking in the morning feeling—
and no doubt looking—like a zombie.

'Why? What have they "done"?'

Her eyes went to his, dazed gold clashing with polished black so sharply that she could almost feel the
sparks that flared between them.

'Was it so very tiring to have me investigated? Did
that snap of your fingers as you sent your minions out
to hunt for scandal—look for something that might incriminate me—wear *you* out? And incriminate me for
what? For pretending to be a maid one night rather than
myself, and possibly get my family into trouble when
you found me roaming about the palace on the night
of the celebration? Dear me, you must have had long,
sleepless nights planning and organising all that!'

To her astonishment Nabil's response was the exact
opposite of what she had been expecting. He laughed.
He threw his head back and laughed loudly, the move-

ment exposing the long, bronzed line of his throat below the rich, black beard, deepening the vee at the opening of his unbuttoned shirt so that her eyes were inevitably drawn over the tanned skin and down to where the crisp black hairs on his chest were revealed.

Since they had arrived at the mountain palace, he had abandoned the formal robes he wore when in the capital and adopted a more relaxed way of dressing, in jeans and a casual shirt. The way that the worn denim clung to his long legs and lean hips, belted close around his narrow waist, had set her pulse racing; but now the sight of him with his head thrown back, his chest expanding with laughter while his hands were pushed deep into the side pockets of his jeans, made her feel as if her legs might melt beneath her.

'I had sleepless nights all right, lady,' he managed at last when the laughter subsided and he caught his breath, eyes bright with amusement as he looked at her. 'But they weren't from planning any investigation into your behaviour.'

'Then—what?'

Was she really that naïve? Nabil had to ask himself. Was it possible that she could actually be unaware of the effect she had on him, the way that he found it impossible to focus on anything but her if they were in the same room together? Had she really not noticed the way that he never slept at night, that he read or watched TV turned down low, or tossed and turned in a painful effort to force himself to stay where he was on the couch and not get up and make his way to the other room where she slept in his bed? Hellfire, was she so damned lucky that she slept too deeply to even be aware that he was so close?

'I saw no sign of these sleepless nights you're claiming. After all, by the time I got up and came out of the bedroom, the bedding on the couch was always folded and packed away...'

'Exactly,' Nabil cut in. 'Do you think I wanted anyone to know how it was with us? To ruin your reputation with everyone there—let them think you were not to be trusted when I had no proof of that? If I was wrong—which I was—then I had to make sure you and I could start again, with no taint of distrust over our marriage.'

If I was wrong—which I was... The words rose up inside her like a golden bubble. Too fragile, too precious, so that she was afraid it might burst if she even looked at it too closely. She needed to hear the words; had to have them said out loud.

'Tell me,' she persisted. 'What was it that kept you from sleeping?'

'Just you.'

The look she turned on him from those golden eyes was so blatantly sceptical and yet tinged with a tiny hint of something that Nabil wanted to be fool enough to call interest glowing in the amber depths.

'You expect me to believe that?'

'It's the...'

Unexpectedly the word failed him. He wanted to be able to assert that it was the truth and nothing but, but there was no way he was going to admit that bruised pride had had a part in his sleeplessness, as well as everything else.

The newly woken physical hunger that tormented his days, heated his nights, was bad enough but the realisation that he had allowed the shadows of the past to reach out and enfold him, just when he had thought that he was freeing himself from them, had stirred the mix to toxic proportions.

He had wanted to believe her—hell, deep in his soul he had known she *was* innocent of the black suspicions that had risen up between them. But it was the fact that he wanted it so much that had forced him to take a step back and reconsider. He had rushed into marriage with Sharmila on just that assumption. With Aziza he had to get it right or it would ruin both himself and his country.

'You think I was happy to settle and sleep after that night?' he demanded, going on to the attack to hide the restless, scrambled thoughts inside his head.

'You were the one who told me I was to sleep alone,' Aziza pointed out now, making him curse his memories and the fact that he couldn't deny her accusation.

In his dreams—in the rare times of sleep he managed—he could still taste the intoxicating blend of sugar from the grapes and the provocation that was pure Aziza, and his hands still burned from the intimacy of the search she had subjected herself to. A search that had had nothing to do with calm common sense and everything that came from need and desire—a desire that was still frustrated. And that was only his fault.

Stiff-necked pride had stopped him from admitting the truth. That he had made a mistake from the first, and regretted it in less than the space of a heartbeat afterwards. Sharmila's toxic legacy still lingered so heavily, throwing black shadows over everything he did, and he had to rid himself of it before he could make a move into the future he had planned for himself.

But at the same time, by keeping him from the burning sexual fulfilment that he had known was just waiting for him in this woman's bed, it had opened up another personal form of hell that had tormented his nights and shadowed his days.

Had he waited too long? Had he pushed Aziza too

hard so that she was too far away from him ever to win back?

'I'm sorry, Aziza,' he said softly and the quiet use of her name seemed to drag her back from wherever her thoughts had drifted to. He saw her blink just once, slowly and thoughtfully, and then she lifted her head and turned to face him.

'I was never asleep either,' she said, stunning him so that his eyes narrowed sharply.

'What are you saying?'

'What do you want me to say, sire?' she challenged him, her chin coming up in the defiant way that always hit him right in the guts. 'That I was only waiting for you to get those reports you asked for so that you would know it was safe to be with me? Did I have any choice? Don't you think it would have been fairer—more reasonable—to check me out *before* you married me? So that we could have had our wedding night uninterrupted—in peace?'

'Yes.' He nodded slowly, never taking his eyes from her face.

A shake of her head sent the black silk of her hair flying, sliding over her face for a moment. The scent of its freshly washed softness caught on his senses, making his body ache. He could command her to come to him, he reflected. He could crook that finger again and insist that she come to him, as his wife, as his subject, but that was not how he wanted this. He wanted her to come to him of her own choice, her free will. He wanted her to hunger for him as much as he desired her, but he wanted her to crave him as a man, rather than a king. It was an odd feeling; one that made him feel strangely vulnerable in a way he had never known before.

'So why didn't you?'

'I was a fool.'

Which one of them had moved? Aziza wondered. She knew she had taken a step forward, maybe two, unable to resist the invisible magnetic pull of his body on hers. But surely she hadn't come so much closer to him as she was now, within touching reach, so that if she just put out a hand...

Her fingers tangled with Nabil's, hard and warm, and a moment later she was pulled against him, the breath crashing from her lungs as she was crushed up against his chest. Her head went back, lifting her mouth to his, her eyes closing as she felt his lips take hers and she gave herself up to the sensation.

It was nothing like the kiss on the balcony. Or the feeling in Nabil's room while she'd struggled with the veil that had concealed her face. That had had all the excitement of a new discovery, of tumbling into an un-expected hunger, an irrepressible need. It had been breathless and greedy, bewildering.

This hunger had been six days brewing. The wait-ing, the isolation, the separation, had left it to feed on itself so that it had grown, wild and blazing. They were both starving, desperate to finish what they had started on their wedding night, and what long hours apart in the heated darkness had built into an uncontrollable longing.

It was so very different somehow, but Aziza couldn't put a name to what had changed. It was only when Nabil muttered, rough and low against her skin, that she realised.

'Wife,' he murmured, the heat of his breath feather-ing the curls of her ear.

She had never heard that note in his voice before and now, finally, she recognised it for what it was.

Trust.

It was just a little word. Just five letters, but it meant so much, changed so much. It meant that whatever darkness had shadowed Nabil's thoughts of her at the beginning—on that first terrifying night they had spent together and yet so far apart—that darkness was now gone. He trusted her, wanted her, and she couldn't ask for more.

His hands seemed to be everywhere, his lips following their path along her skin. She was stroked, caressed, tantalised, tormented, coming alive under his hands, plunging hard and fast and deep into what it meant to be a woman who was wanted by a man. And how it felt to be the woman who wanted the man she was with so much that she was out of her head with need.

'My wife,' Nabil muttered again, his voice dark and thick as he swung her up into his arms and carried her from the room and up the curving marble staircase to kick open the door into the bedroom. Never once in the whole of that hasty journey did his lips leave hers, his body making the climb surefooted and safely even though he was acting blind.

In the bedroom he dropped her down on to the cushioned softness of the bed, leaning over her as he did so to tangle his hands in her hair, pull her face up to his again for yet more of those overwhelming, demanding kisses. Until, in the space of a heartbeat it seemed, kisses were not enough and his hands plundered her body, the heat of his palms branding her as his with every touch.

'You are wearing too many clothes.'

He ripped the soft, green silk tunic open down the front, baring her breasts to his burning eyes. A moment later, both sides of the top fell away, slithering to the floor to pool at her feet, to be joined just moments later by the white trousers she had been wearing, her underwear tossed aside with a total indifference to where it fell.

Then he was there beside her on the bed, his own clothes discarded alongside hers, the heat and hardness of his lean length stoking the fires that were already running wild through her yearning body. His kisses were more intimate now, lingering on each breast to swirl his tongue around the pouting nipples, drawing them into the heated cavern of his mouth and suckling hard until she was crying out with need.

But he was ahead of her there too, stroking his way down the length of her body and parting her legs, finding the most intimate part of her and making a raw, rough sound of satisfaction as his fingers encountered the moisture that told how ready she was for him there.

But then, just when she could least bear it, he suddenly hesitated and paused, looking down into her face. His eyes were glazed with passion, a heated blush streaking across high cheekbones above the rich growth of beard, but he held himself still for a moment, letting her know without words just what he was thinking. He was considering her inexperience; thinking of the need for care.

But care and consideration were not what Aziza wanted—not what she needed.

'No!' she ordered, her voice raw and high with a need that matched his. 'Don't stop now. Don't!'

'No chance, lady.'

Her legs were pushed apart by the pressure of his powerful thighs as he settled himself between them, the heat of his length coming up against the point where she most yearned for him. Fearful that he might hesitate once more, she found herself acting on instincts as old as time, lifting her hips slightly and opening herself to him until, on a groan that was a mixture of triumph and surrender, he gave himself up to the passion that controlled him, pressing in and up until he possessed her completely.

The sting of pain was only brief and soon forgotten as from then it was all fire and fury, passion and need taking over and driving every last thought from her mind. She didn't know where she ended and Nabil began, only that they were together and together they were storming higher, higher, reaching for something she had never known existed but felt that now she would die if she never achieved it.

Just seconds later she felt that she *was* dying. Of pleasure; of the brilliance of the delight that was exploding along every nerve in her body, sending her spinning over the edge into a freefall into space. All that she was aware of was the fact that Nabil went with her, following her along the same blazing path, with her name a raw, broken sound of triumph on his lips as he did so.

A long, mindless time later, Nabil's breathing finally slowed and he stirred at last, stretching luxuriously and pulling her close so that she was curved against him, skin to skin, her slender, smooth legs tangled with the bronzed length of his, dark hairs rough against her sensitive skin.

He cupped a hand under her chin to lift her face towards his, a frown drawing his black brows together.

'Are you all right? It was your first time. Are you OK?'

For several seconds Aziza had to struggle to speak. She found that she was blushing fierily at the ease with which he had realised her inexperience. Had it showed? Had she disappointed him?

'Disappointed? Did it look that way?'

To her horror she realised that she had spoken the words out loud, letting them escape in a whisper from a tongue she seemed to have no control over.

'How could you be a disappointment?'

'Well—I have nothing to compare it with. You might have wanted more—seduction on my part.'

'More seduction?' To her consternation the amusement was back in his eyes, making them glitter behind the rich thickness of his black lashes. 'Now, why would I need that?'

One powerful hand smoothed over her body, down from her shoulders and over her ribcage, lingering on her hips. Aziza fought with herself not to respond too naively, too revealingly, even as her insides seemed to melt under his touch, turning her stomach into a pit of warm honey, the moisture between her thighs drying against the heat of her skin. She wanted to press herself against that heated caress, purr like a contented kitten. But even as the thought slid into her mind she felt the raw, hungry pulse start to beat again between her legs, making her shift restlessly against the sheets.

'You are pure seduction in yourself. I knew from day one that it would be like this.'

'And would that be day one when I was your chosen wife? Or at the banquet following our—'

'Neither,' Nabil broke in sharply, his eyes fixed on where the long hands rested, lean and slightly darker against the cushioned curve of her hip. 'I wanted you that first night, when we met.'

Aziza's breath caught, and had to be forced out again in a rush. She felt as if the colour that she could feel rushing into her cheeks must be flooding the rest of her body, leaving her flushed pink against the whiteness of the sheets.

'When I was…'

Nabil shifted slightly in the bed, moving so that he was looking straight down into her eyes. His hand moved from her thigh to cup the side of her cheek, warm and gentle.

'Zia the maid, or Aziza my princess, you were the one who stirred my senses more than any other woman I was supposed to consider as my bride.'

But not any woman, ever, a cold little voice whispered inside Aziza's head. There had been Sharmila, his first love, the mother of his child. The woman who had died in his arms. She was only here because of the tragedy that had filled his youth.

In a marriage that was the result of love, such as the one that Nabil had shared with Sharmila, this was the time that, in the darkness and softness of the marriage bed, he would have whispered words of love, of joy that she was his wife and they were together. But there was no room for feelings such as that in this marriage that was made purely from diplomacy and political alliances. No matter what she felt for Nabil, those feelings were not returned. But at least he had chosen her as his bride. And he wanted her.

'I felt that way too,' she grabbed at all her courage to admit. 'From the moment you kissed me.'

Oh, who was she kidding? Before that kiss, long before it, she had given him her heart. He'd had it in his keeping ever since she'd first seen him, even though he'd held it so carelessly, not even aware of what he had.

'I lo—' she began, needing to say the words just once, even if he never put any value on them. But in the space of a heartbeat all her courage deserted her and she knew that she couldn't bear to let her secret out into the cold light of day. 'I loved that kiss,' she managed instead. 'And I wanted more.'

Raising herself up on one elbow, she pressed her lips to his, feeling the combination of the soft and the rough as the edges of his beard brushed against her skin. She'd longed to have the nerve to take that kiss up along his cheek, out to the pale, raised line along his cheekbone and out towards his temple.

Tonight she felt brave enough to do that. Lifting herself again, she let her mouth touch on the marked line of his scar, kissing it softly and delicately, letting her tongue trace its way towards the corner of his eye, tasting the salt of his skin and feeling the brush of those long black eyelashes as his eyes closed for a moment against her caress.

'Aziza…'

His voice was rough and raw as if catching against something in his throat, so that hearing it she was already prepared for the way he reached for her, hard fingers clamping around her arms as he pulled her under the weight of his body. Pushing one strong knee between her thighs, he opened her up to him while the heat of his mouth captured her breast, moist tongue trailing up towards the pouting nipple and encircling it, making her writhe in hungry response.

'Does this look like I need more seduction?' he muttered, the words hot against her skin. He adjusted his position so that the thick, hard force of his body pushed at her welcoming core. 'Or *feel* like it?'

He emphasised the words with a swift, powerful thrust, filling her completely and joining them as one.

'This is all I need,' he declared as he began to move,

fierce and strong, and totally obliterating her ability to think any more.

'You…' Aziza managed. 'You're all I need.'

But then she had to break off on a moan of delight, abandoning herself to pleasure before, thankfully, she, or Nabil, could realise that she had meant the words in a very much deeper way.

CHAPTER ELEVEN

WHAT A DIFFERENCE a week could make. Aziza yawned
widely, stretching luxuriously in the bed and feeling
the tiny aches and tender spots that had resulted from
long nights with Nabil.

Long, passionate nights, and even longer, sensuous
days. Nabil had never actually described this trip to
the mountain palace as their honeymoon, but the truth
was that that was exactly what it had turned into. Because, after all, wasn't that what a honeymoon was all
about? About spending time with your new spouse without anything interrupting the private moments? About
having the freedom to discover the sexual delight they
had in each other and indulge in the pleasures of married love?

Not that love had anything to do with it, at least on
Nabil's part. The thought made Aziza flinch and start
into a sitting position. The movement of stretching her
arms wide had brought them into contact with the rest
of the bed, forcing her to the awareness of the emptiness on either side of her.

Hadn't it been this way all week? Every morning she
had woken to find that Nabil had got out of the bed before she stirred, leaving her alone and letting the sheets

where he had lain grow cool and empty without the warmth of his body there.

But this wasn't like all the other times. It was still the middle of the night, the room in darkness. Outside the high windows the only light was the starlit sky, the faintest breeze stirring the delicate curtains the only sign of movement in the silent palace.

Where was he? And what had pulled him from his sleep tonight?

Slipping from the bed, Aziza pushed her feet into soft slippers and pulled a white silky robe on over her nakedness. Padding silently over the cool marble floors, she made her way out of the bedroom, through the royal suite and down the long, silent corridors.

The waft of a breeze from a door left slightly open alerted her to just where Nabil must be. There was a balcony there, smaller and higher than the one outside the banqueting hall of the city palace where she and Nabil had met that first night, but enough like it to have memories of that meeting swirling in her thoughts as she peered through the partially opened door.

'Nab…' she began, but what she saw froze the words on her tongue and had her pulling back slightly, out of sight.

Just as on that first evening, Nabil was leaning against the high wall of the balcony, staring out at the darkened valley below. He had only paused to pull on a pair of jeans, with nothing on his chest or his feet, and the moonshine brushed his powerful shoulders, the long line of his ribcage, with a wash of silver. His face was set and intent, his gaze fixed on some point away on the far horizon, and the dark shadow of his beard could not conceal the tight compression of his mouth, the tension in the muscles of his jaw and throat.

He looked disturbed and alone, so much like the way he had looked that first night. Then she had felt concern and sympathy for him, so much that she had made a move to break into his mental isolation. But tonight she didn't dare to speak, to make any move or sound that would draw his attention to her. Tonight was not the time to break into whatever bleak dreams enclosed him.

Particularly not when she saw him lift his left hand and rub at the white line of the scar on his face, fretting at it with obvious disquiet.

The ghost of tragic Sharmila must have surfaced in his thoughts, possibly even seeming to reprove him for marrying another bride, for sharing the heat of passion in their bed.

There was no way that Aziza wanted to take the risk of being told that Nabil regretted the passion they had shared when it revived memories of the bond he had enjoyed with his tragic young love. Silently, reluctantly, she turned and crept away, leaving Nabil to the darkness of his thoughts.

Perhaps one day she would learn how to handle the changeable moods that this new husband of hers displayed so openly. One moment he would be calm, attentive, considerate. He took her riding out along the mountain paths, or swam in the huge swimming pool, built indoors to hide them from the burning heat of the desert sun. But then in the space of a heartbeat he would change, his disposition becoming darker, withdrawn, and each time he had left her bed she had recognised how hard she found it to reach him.

Once the restraint between them had been stripped away on that first night, from then it had taken just a second to put a light to the hunger that they felt for each other, heating the blood in their veins until they were molten with passion. In the space of a heartbeat they would lose themselves in each other, obliterating reality in the heat they created between them.

But when the burn of passion ebbed, when they lay silent and sated on the cool sheets, as the throb of fulfilment slowly ebbed between Aziza's legs, her pulse slowing to a heavy, lazy beat, she had felt Nabil stirring, raking long fingers through the black sleekness of his hair. It had taken an effort to turn to him, one day, fighting against the wash of exhaustion, the way that her eyes felt as if they were weighted down so that it was impossible to lift her heavy lids at all.

'Where are you going?'

She'd had to make an effort to put no note of complaint into it and, although her hands itched to fasten around the long muscular arms that were now pushing himself up from the mattress, she clamped them tight down by her sides to keep them from reaching for him.

'Things to do,' he'd said, pulling on the trousers that had been discarded on the floor in the heat of their rush to the bed.

'Such as? This is our...' But no, the word 'honeymoon' was obviously going to be a mistake. A red rag to a bull if the swift, flashing glance he'd turned in her direction was anything to go by.

How did someone switch off so completely just like that? She'd been fighting hard against the sleep that had still threatened to overwhelm her, and all she'd wanted was to curl up close to him, to drift away on the warm sea of contentment into the peace of dreams.

Not Nabil. It seemed that, having appeased his appetite, he now no longer wanted to stay around.

She could let it hurt her. Darn it, it *did* hurt, but she had a choice of whether to show it or not. And showing the pain that was twisting in her heart would be to open herself up to him too much. To Nabil she was only his wife of convenience, the chosen one for this arranged marriage. So she would be a fool to expect the richness of love from this relationship.

'You are the most inconsistent creature I've ever met,' she'd teased when he had his face buried in the white T-shirt he was pulling over his head. The drowsiness of completion was ebbing from her now and she pulled the fine white sheet up around her, coiling into it as he turned to face her.

'And why do you think that is?' Nabil responded. 'Have you considered what part you might play in making me like this?'

'You mean you never were so unpredictable before?'

'Not that anyone has told me.'

'But would they actually tell you—hmm?' Aziza couldn't help coming back at him. 'I mean you are the Sheikh, after all. Who would dare to risk their head by telling His Great High Majesty that his moods were... erratic?'

'You might be describing my father,' Nabil growled. 'But I am not him.'

'True,' Aziza had to concede. 'Sheikh Omar—was very much of the old school. Male power was dominant and women were very much second-class citizens. In his day, I certainly wouldn't be able to have my driving licence.'

'You can drive? Then you must pick out a car you would like and I'll make sure it's yours. That is unless you would prefer to have the royal chauffeur drive you everywhere.'

'Oh, no—you're mixing me up with Jamalia! She'd

be happy to have a private chauffeur—but I'd feel trapped, imprisoned.'

'Then I cannot have my wife feeling like a prisoner. I've not spent the last ten years dragging Rhastaan into the twenty-first century to let that happen.'

And yet you were prepared to go through with a traditionally arranged marriage, Aziza reflected. Once again it seemed that Nabil was a blend of enlightened and primitive. It was a heady combination, one that made her blood heat just to think of it.

The man who stood before her, black hair ruffled, in a loose white T-shirt worn with battered denim jeans, his long, tanned bare feet placed firmly on the ornately woven rug, could never be just 'any man'. He stood so tall and proud, his dark head held arrogantly high, and there was the burn of knowledge in those obsidian eyes. Knowledge of who he was and why he was here. Knowledge of his position of power and honour. He wore the casual clothes as magnificently as if they'd been the richest ceremonial robes. He was a man born to be King and he needed none of the trappings of state to prove it.

'You've certainly instituted some great changes,' she said quietly.

'Ones that were badly needed.'

Nabil's nod of agreement was dark, sombre-faced. But then how could it be anything else when they were treading on a dangerous, rocky road here? Talking about the reforms that Nabil had implemented in Rhastaan since he had come to the throne meant recalling the rebellion in the country that had risen up against his father, and had still been bubbling underneath like lava just waiting to erupt from a volcano when Nabil had inherited the throne.

It had been his father's entrenched attitudes that had

created the mood of rebellion, and possibly had led to the fact that Nabil had had to inherit the crown unexpectedly early when the helicopter carrying his parents had crashed into a mountainside, killing them both. He had only been nineteen then.

Remembering how she had felt when she had been thrown into the public arena, she looked back at that nineteen-year-old—little more than a boy—with a sense of sympathy.

'Had your father taught you how to be a king? Did he show you what was needed, talk about what you should do?'

'He expected me to learn by example. To wait and watch.'

Nabil didn't have to say anything more about the coldness and the distance he had felt from his father. It was there in the bleakness of his tone, the clouded focus of his eyes on to the distance.

'I expect that he never thought that he would die so early and he believed I was too young—too immature— to take on the duties of the King.'

He pushed one hand roughly through his hair, leaving it wildly ruffled.

'He was probably right about that then. I was hell-bent on fighting against my destiny if I possibly could. My father found me irresponsible and a most unsatisfactory son. You must know how that feels.'

Aziza nodded slowly, stunned that he had taken in so much of her story about being the 'spare'.

'But my father only neglected to prepare me for an important marriage—there wasn't a country that I needed to learn how to rule.'

'But, if I'd followed his example, then I believe civil

war would have torn the country apart very soon after I came to the throne.'

'You inherited a difficult and dangerous legacy. And you had no one to share it with.'

'I thought I had.' Nabil raked his hands through his hair once more, the gesture giving away the discomfort of his thoughts. 'But that was not to be.'

It was that rebellion that had led to the assassination attempt. All these years later that rebellion was still reaching out its tentacles as it touched her life now. Because, without it, Nabil would have been married and a father a long time ago. Like Prince Karim and his beautiful Clementina, he and Sharmila would have been celebrating their tenth anniversary, with the young crown prince or princess coming close to celebrating their ninth birthday. Her heart ached in two separate ways just to think of it.

Because, if that had been so, where would she be? Not here in the mountain palace, with the King, her husband, newly risen from her bed. She would no doubt still be at home with her parents and sister, acting as Jamalia's chaperone, enduring her father's slights.

'Perhaps…' It was a struggle to get the words from a throat that was dry with nerves, but she had to say them. 'Perhaps we could start again with that too. I know I haven't had the right sort of training…'

'Training isn't everything,' Nabil put in sharply. 'My mother was brought up in the belief that one day she would be Queen. None of that made a blind bit of difference when she was expected to do any public duties. More often than not, she just didn't turn up. You must have attended more official events in the last couple of weeks than she did in a year.'

He had told her she'd done well and that gave her the

courage to speak the words that were burning on her tongue, put there by the loneliness, the isolation, she had seen in him just moments before.

'I am your wife and if I can be of any help at all...'

She'd started out bravely but faltered to a halt under the impact of his polished jet stare. Was that approval or the exact opposite? At last Nabil nodded his head slowly.

'Perhaps...' But then abruptly his mood changed as he frowned sharply. 'What's that on your neck?'

He followed up the harsh demand by grabbing a large hand mirror, ornately backed in gold, and holding it up so that she could see her own reflection.

'That?' Aziza's hands went to her throat, touching the red marks there and on her cheeks lightly. 'It's nothing.'

'It certainly wasn't there last night.'

'It wasn't,' Aziza admitted, a rush of blood along her skin making more of her face colour red. 'Because it was last night—and this afternoon—that put it there... It was your beard that marked my skin.'

She watched his long fingers rub up against his beard, brush through the crisp black hair.

'I'm sorry.' He sounded it. 'I never meant to harm you.'

'No harm,' she assured him. 'It's not your fault that I have such appallingly sensitive skin. But don't worry.' Encouraged by this new approachable mood, she took a couple of steps forward to reach up and touch his face. 'I know why you grew that beard—to conceal this.'

Gently she smoothed soft fingers over the long line of the scar then jumped as he reacted fast and unexpectedly, capturing her hand and bringing it down sharply.

'Don't!'

'I'm sorry. I didn't realise it still hurts.'

'Not hurts' was his growling response. 'At least, not in that way.'

* * *

The physical pain had healed long ago, Nabil thought, rubbing his scar, as the first red fingers of the dawn warmed the balcony where he had spent half the night. Other scars were not so easy to deal with. Least of all the fact that the mark on his face was only there because Sharmila had had him wrapped around her delicate fingers. Led by the lethal combination of loneliness and the adolescent sexual hunger she'd been able to create in him, he had lost all ability to think straight. She had persuaded him to do exactly as she wanted and it was only when the truth had dawned cold and dark that he'd had to face how blind he had been.

It wasn't like that with Aziza. He had chosen her, married her, because he had been looking for peace and calm after the years of tension that had followed from his mistakes where Sharmila was concerned. He'd spent the ten years making up to his country for the errors of his wild, selfish youth and had believed that the younger, gentler sister of the El Afarim family would help him do that.

And give him children. The heir he needed.

Instead he had found himself on a roller-coaster ride where nothing was as he had imagined it. Where he had expected to be a dutiful king, a respectful husband, he had never anticipated the brutal punch of suspicion that was the toxic legacy Sharmila had left behind. But even as he had doubted, suspected, wanted to reject, he had known that he could not do any of those things.

The one clear, unquestioning thought had been that he wanted Aziza in his bed. He had done from the start, from that moment when he had seen her on the balcony and, now he knew the reality of the passion they shared, he wanted her more than ever. The nights they had enjoyed here in the mountain palace had only added to that hunger. The one-night stands he had indulged in had done little to truly satisfy; he wanted so much more than that. And he had found it in Aziza's arms, Aziza's bed, Aziza's body. Each night he spent with her gave him all he had been looking for physically—and more. But it was nothing like the temporary oblivion he had once sought. Instead he was left with a sense of completion and fulfilment that, when it ebbed away, left him hungrier than ever before. Wanting more, needing her in a way that he could see no hope of ever satisfying.

No sooner had he left her bed than he wanted to be back in it. Back in her arms, deep inside her welcoming body. It was a hunger that swirled and boiled inside him now as he pushed himself away from the balcony wall, knowing he had to go and find her once again. He came back to the bedroom, chilled and stiff after the long time he had spent staring out into the darkness of the night. Back to the warmth and softness of her bed. The warmth and softness of her.

But in the doorway he could only pause, unable to go any further. Much as he wanted to, he couldn't bring himself to wake her.

How many nights had this happened? How many times had he stood here like this and watched her sleep? With her jet-black hair splayed out over the pillows, her eyes closed, the long, feathering lashes creating a soft, dark arc across the fine cheekbones? She looked so young—so peaceful—so innocent. Was this what her child would look like? A child that would be half hers and half his—truly *his* this time? He had thought he wanted that child before, but now the hunger for it caught in his heart and took root.

A sigh escaped those full, rose-tinted lips, and as he

watched she moved slightly, shifting against the pillows.
She tossed her head slightly, murmuring something in
her sleep, and he saw once again those red marks on
her cheeks and throat, and lower down where the silken
robe she was wearing gaped over her breasts.

Those marks looked even worse against the softness
of her skin, making him wince at the sight of them. He
had thought that he had made sure he would never mark
her again like that. He'd shaved off the dark growth of
beard that he'd worn like a defence since the day he
had learned the truth of Sharmila's betrayal, wishing
he could wash the past down the drain with the hairs.
But it seemed that the stubble that grew again during
the day only made matters worse. There was no getting away from what happened, no removing all he'd
hidden from her.

He longed to get back into that bed again, to gather
her up into his arms and lose himself in her, but that
was not the answer. He doubted that there was an answer. So he turned slowly and silently and walked away,
heading for the office where there were always docu-
ments and affairs of state that demanded his attention.
In the past he had always been able to lose himself in
the details of government, blotting out everything else.
But it seemed there was no blocking out Aziza. She
had well and truly got under his skin and he couldn't
push away thoughts of her. She was there in his mind
all day, every day.

CHAPTER TWELVE

SOMEHOW AFTER LONG hours lying awake, waiting for Nabil to come back to bed, Aziza managed to go back to sleep and when she woke again the morning had dawned clear and bright. But the space beside her in the bed where Nabil had lain was empty and so cold that it was obvious he had never returned to her at any point after she had seen him on the balcony. He shared her bed only when he wanted, when he was looking for sex, and after that he moved away, leaving her alone.

That thought left her feeling disturbingly vulnerable. It was as if he was some long ago conqueror who visited his concubine only at night.

She shouldn't let it get to her; after all, she knew that was what this marriage was about, why she was here. She had thought that she could cope with it. But when she thought that she and Nabil had taken some steps forward, towards each other, the restlessness was like an itch in her brain that told her she would struggle to do so. She wanted more. Needed more. It was a need that had taken a long time to grow, slowly coming to the surface so that she could really look at it.

If she had a child, hers and Nabil's, then as its mother she would hold it first in her heart. But would the love she had for her child be enough? Where could she turn to for the real strength of adult love? The difference between what she had felt for Nabil as a child and the way she felt now told her that was vital for her happiness in the future.

Restless and unsettled, she flung herself out of the bed and snatched up a towel, heading for the swimming pool to work off some of the edgy energy that made her skin prickle. It was only when she reached the pool, with its inviting water lapping at the edges of the blue and green tiles, that she realised that she hadn't brought any sort of a swimming costume with her.

'Oh, what does it matter?' she muttered aloud.

She needed exercise, needed something to stop the crazy whirling of her thoughts, the uncomfortable edgy feeling that tormented her.

She didn't need a costume; there was no one here to see her.

Not even the husband who only visited her for sex, and left her alone all the rest of the night.

The thought drove her into a high, soaring dive, plunging into the pool and striking out for the far end in a fast, furious crawl. The coolness of the water soothed her burning skin, and the speed of the exercise burned away some of the edginess that plagued her. It was only when her muscles began to tire that she slowed and headed for the side of the pool once again. Only to pull up sharply when she became aware of the tall, powerful figure sitting on the tiled edge. Long, tanned legs hung down into the water, black hairs plastered against his skin as she emerged, hanging on to the side.

'Someone after you?' Nabil drawled lazily as she looked up into his face. A face that was still slightly unfamiliar without the black growth of beard. The scar that marked his cheekbone stood out brutally now, spotlighted by a ray of sun that slashed through the windows. 'You looked as if you were escaping from a demon from hell.'

The demons in her own mind, Aziza told herself, starting to lift herself out of the pool then immediately letting herself drop back into the concealing water as she became aware of her nakedness.

'I just needed the exercise.'

She hoped that he would take her breathlessness as being the result of her exertions rather than the effect his appearance was having on her. He had obviously come to swim but, unlike her, he was actually wearing a pair of sleek black swimming shorts. There was so much satiny bronze skin on show that Aziza felt as if the water around her had heated to boiling point, all the cooling she'd aimed for destroyed in a jolting heartbeat. It was foolish to feel any embarrassment at the thought of him seeing her nakedness when he had explored every inch of her body throughout the night. But the heavy sensuality of the bedroom made sharing her body with his so much more intimate and private than here, in the burning light of the day.

'I think we could have found another more enjoyable way to burn off all that energy, *habibti*.'

The black eyes gleamed with heightened awareness, the warmth of his smile like a caress in itself as it slid over her burning face, down to where her breasts, swaying in the rippling water, were clearly visible just below the surface.

'So you've finished all your other important business?'

The assessing, sidelong glance he turned on her had her curling her toes against the patterned tiles on the floor of the pool. She was revealing too much of her secret feelings and by doing so was making herself vulnerable in ways he wouldn't even be able to guess at.

This is our honeymoon, were the words she longed to fling at him. He had never actually described this stay at the mountain palace as a honeymoon; it was only in her foolish heart that she had allowed the words to slide in and take root.

'You married a king.' The reminder was low, laced with a deadly intent that shivered over her exposed skin. 'There are always those demands on my time. Day or *night*.'

She didn't need the pointed emphasis on the last word. If it really had been the affairs of state that had taken him from her bed, she could have had no complaint. But last night had shown her that it was nothing so demanding that had disturbed his sleep, making him abandon her. It was some darkness in his own mind, some memory, and she could have little doubt just who had been in his thoughts.

'So are you feeling rather neglected, my bride?' Nabil enquired in a very different tone. 'Do I not pay you enough attention?'

Not enough for someone who wanted a meeting of minds and hearts as well as the fiery connection their bodies shared. Not enough for someone who had started to realise that the love she had given to this man when she was just a child was still in his possession. And that that love was a one-way street with nothing coming back at her.

'You—' she began but the words were broken off, snatched back, as Nabil made a sudden move, reaching down from where he sat, hooking his hands under her arms. A moment later he had lifted her out of the pool, water sluicing down her body as he raised her

high enough to sit on his lap, the warmth of his skin
against her naked body, the sleek tightness of the swimming shorts, doing nothing to hide the power and heat
of his desire.

'Nabil!' Aziza gasped, but the word was crushed
back down into her mouth as Nabil took her lips in a
hard, demanding kiss that pressed them open, let in his
marauding tongue, setting up a wild, erotic dance as he
took her mouth, tasted her, tantalised her.

His hands were all over her body, hot against her
water-cooled skin, stroking, caressing, hard palms cup-
ping and enclosing her breasts, making her writhe in
heated response to his burning touch.

'Does this feel like neglect, my lovely wife?' he muttered against her mouth, trailing his kisses down and
along the lines of her throat. 'Is this what I've not done
enough of to please you?'

'No…'

It was a shaken moan. At the juncture of her thighs
the pressure of his desire was making her hot and restless so that she shifted against him, hearing his groan
of hungered response as his fingers tightened, bruising, around her arms.

'If you want more then you only have to ask,' Nabil
muttered against her throat, lowering his face to taste
the velvet texture of her breasts where the water drops
glistened like diamonds against the smooth honey
colour of her skin. 'Hell, you don't even have to ask…'

It was what *he* wanted, Nabil acknowledged. The
only thing on his mind since he'd arrived at the pool just
in time to see her toss aside the white robe and raise her
arms, lifting those soft, perfect breasts as she posed on
the edge of the pool. The sunlight had gilded the golden
tones of her flesh, the jet darkness of her hair flowing

down on to her shoulders just for a moment before she had pushed off from the side, diving in a perfect arc into the clear, cool water.

His heart had pounded just at the sight of her, the hard, hungry tightening of his body pushing against the restriction of the swimming shorts, demanding release. His first impulse had been to plunge into the pool after her, to chase her down, capture her and haul her up against him, to turn the clear depths of the pool into a heated, sensual playground with her glorious body slippery as a seal against him. But a rush of second thoughts had him pausing, waiting, watching; letting the pulse of desire grow and heat as it beat against his temples, throbbed its way down his body. Sometimes anticipation was half of the pleasure.

If this was what she wanted then this he could give her. This was what he knew how to offer, where he found no complications, no hidden dangers lurking in it like black, jagged rocks at the bottom of a smooth, clear sea. This was the way that they could communicate without any doubts, any problems, the way that took all thought from his mind and gave him up to the oblivion...

No! For a moment he found himself stiffening in shock. For the first time he realised fully how things had been changing since this woman had come into his life.

Because it was *this* that he wanted. This feeling of connection, of sensation, of being alive. It was not oblivion he was looking for but the continuation of this life force—the way of prolonging it, making it grow. He wanted it more. He wanted it now.

He wanted it for ever.

Shifting on the cool, damp tiles, he lifted Aziza so that she was sitting astride him, long, smooth legs

splayed out on either side of his. The contrast between
the black hairs that hazed his thighs and the silky skin
on hers was an erotic dream all of its own and the added
enticement of the small triangle of curls at the point
where she was most intimately close to his body was
almost more than he could bear.

'My Queen,' he said, rough and raw. 'My beautiful Queen.'

For some reason his words made her stiffen in his
arms, pulling slightly away from him, her deep eyes
strangely clouded, and silently he cursed the father who
had done such a job of making her feel second best.

'Do you doubt it? Does this not tell you what I think
of you?'

Lifting his hips, he pressed the swell of his erec-
tion against the most intimate spot between her spread
legs, almost undoing himself completely when he did.
Fiercely he fought back the groan of need, of hunger,
that almost escaped him.

'Or this?' he muttered against her partly opened
mouth, taking her lips in a hard, fiercely passionate
kiss. A kiss that took him to the edge and very nearly
pushed him right over it, kicking into his heart in a way
that made it skip several hungry beats.

'See…?' he muttered, holding up his hands so that
she could see the way they shook, the way his fingers
trembled with the need to touch her, with every part of
her body giving him the nourishment he needed in the
same moment that it deepened and increased the hunger she created in him.

'Oh, yes…and what about this?' Aziza's echo of response was just a whisper as she leaned forward and
pressed her breasts tight against his chest.

It was all that was needed to destroy what was left

of his control, the explosion inside his head taking him out of reality and into a world where there was only her, only her warm, yielding body and the inferno of desire they were creating between them.

Shifting awkwardly on the blue tiles, he managed to get one hand between them, tugging down the clinging shorts, the moist curls at the junction of her thighs brushing against the back of his hand as he did so. The black Lycra slipped into the pool as he let it drop and, free from the constraint, his desire was hard and strong immediately, pressing against her so much that all she had to do was to make a small shift in her position to offer him entry, take him into her.

It felt like coming home. He almost lost himself right there and then but Aziza was not going to settle for hard and fast. Instead she clenched her inner muscles around him, sliding slowly down on to his hungry length and he felt her mouth curve into a smile against him as his breath caught sharply in his throat.

'Is this what you mean?'

Her voice was a smoky murmur, coiling around him. 'Or this?'

She gave a wicked little twist of her hips, reducing him to a groaning wreck as he let her take charge, closing his eyes and holding tight to what little control he had left. The sensation of her breasts against his chest, her hands in his hair, while all the time her secret muscles stroked and tightened, drawing him out of himself and into a world of pure sensation such as he had never felt before.

'Aziza…' he managed, raw and rough, and felt the unexpected laughter that shook her slender form.

'I know,' she assured him, whispering against his ear, her breath warm on his skin. 'Believe me, I know.'

She abandoned her tormenting seduction and clamped her hands over his shoulders so as to give herself support as she gave in to the need that was burning in her too and took him higher, higher...

Until, with her name a choking cry on his lips, he gave himself up to the sensation, losing himself, his mind seeming to explode in the same moment that his body abandoned all control and let the hot, fierce essence of his seed pump into her as she too gave a loud, keening cry of fulfilment.

A long time later his mind came back into his body, his heart rate easing to a point where he could actually breathe again. But he still couldn't see or even hear anything but the jagged breathing of the woman who sat astride him, her head limp against his shoulder, her internal muscles still holding him, her shudders of completion slowing, ebbing away.

'So now...'

It was the only sound his tongue was capable of. The only thought his mind could manage. All he could focus on was her, Aziza, his wife, the woman who had just obliterated all awareness of anything but her as he'd lost himself in her.

'Now do you see why I chose you?'

He was getting control of his breath, snatching in great gulps of air as his heart rate eased, his chest stopped heaving.

'And they thought I might choose your sister.'

Aziza's smooth body suddenly stiffened against him. He didn't recognise her withdrawal so much as feel the way that her head lifted slightly, leaving a small cooling spot on his shoulder, a tiny movement dragging the wet silk of her hair across his skin.

'I would have been crazy to do that when you're all woman.'

He stirred slightly, enjoying the sensation as he moved her body against his, the way her legs still held him. At the same time he stroked his hands down from her shoulders and along the length of her spine, spreading out at the base to curve over her hips.

'Curves in the right places...'

He was already hungry for her again, hardening, thickening, pressing against her. If he carried her to the bedroom they could take up where they had left off—in a lot more comfort.

'Child-bearing hips.'

Too late he realised that his sensual daydream was not shared. Aziza's body was taut and distant; her fine bones as brittle as glass as she held herself away from him. Once more he caressed her hips but felt her instant and unbelievable rejection.

'No!' She scrambled from him, slightly clumsy in her unexpected haste to be free.

He reached up, tried to grab her hand, but she dodged his reaching fingers, twisting free from the awkward half-grasp he managed.

'No!' she said again, her head down, black hair hiding her face as she whirled away, dashing for the doorway, fleeing out and down the corridor before he had even registered that she had got away from him.

What the devil had got into her? He had made it plain that he desired her like a crazy man. He'd even *said* it, for goodness' sake! But she had turned from him and run as if he had suddenly sprouted horns. Pushing himself to his feet, he set off after her.

It seemed that he and his wife needed to talk—really talk.

CHAPTER THIRTEEN

CHILD-BEARING HIPS...

The words rang inside Aziza's head as she dashed down the long corridors, thankful that she didn't meet any member of the palace staff before she reached the safety of her suite—*Nabil's* suite.

Be honest, she reproved herself bitterly. She didn't own anything inside this marriage; it all belonged to Nabil. And she was here for one reason—and one reason only. She was expected to provide the King with his vital heirs. That was the reason he had picked her instead of her sister. She knew that so why should she expect anything more from this man who was her husband? The man she had been fool enough to allow her own heart to open up and fall in love with.

And that was where the problem had its roots. She had gone to the pool in an attempt to get away from her thoughts, to try to accept what she had and not look for more. But she wanted more.

In a lifetime of being the second child, the 'other daughter', the one who was always supposed to wait in line, she hadn't recognised the deepest need until it surfaced. She'd even let herself think that being chosen above her sister, placed above her parents, would lift her, give her the sense of fulfilment that she needed.

But now she knew that even being first of all women in the country wasn't enough. It would never be enough. She needed to be first in someone's heart. Knowing that she was not could only end up breaking her own heart. The loud bang as she slammed the door to the bedroom shut resounded all through the palace, and yet she knew it was only an empty gesture. There was no way she could close it against Nabil, or shut him out. Like everything else in his world, Nabil owned that door, the key that locked it. They all belonged to him.

And so did she.

Just when she had admitted to herself how much she wanted more, Nabil had brought it right back down to basics again. She had to face the fact that she was little more to him than one of the beautiful pure-bred Arab horses in his stables. A brood mare. Of full value only when she was pregnant with his heir—to give good value from those 'child-bearing hips'!

She had to pull herself together. She had no doubt that he would come after her. She had given away too much already by reacting as she had done; she couldn't let him see how much his words had upset her. A bronze-coloured tunic and black leggings lay on a chair beside the bed and she snatched them up on her way past. The bathroom door at least could be locked from the inside.

In here, she could take a little time to make some vital repairs to her appearance, she told herself, staring in horror at the wild disarray of her hair, the huge pools that were her eyes with disturbing, bruised-looking shadows under them. That sight if nothing else drew a dark, emphatic line under the turmoil that burned in her heart. Could she accept what Nabil and all the rest of the world thought of as the huge amount she had been offered when deep inside she knew it was too little, could never be enough?

She barely had time swiftly to shower, dry and pull on the clothes, drag a comb painfully through the knots in her hair and tie it back with a band before she heard footsteps in the bedroom. A moment later Nabil's fist hit the bathroom door with a force that almost shook the room.

'Aziza! Come out now. What the hell are you doing in there?'

'I thought I'd better get dressed,' she bluffed as she turned the key and opened the door, leaning in the open space in what she hoped was a relaxed pose. She didn't want to make him probe too deeply into why she had reacted as she had. He would see through the carefully protective mask she had shown him since their wedding day if she didn't take care. 'I suddenly worried that someone might find us.'

'Very suddenly,' was Nabil's dry response. 'You should know that no one would disturb us without my permission.'

'Of course. That is how it always is for you, isn't it? But I haven't lived with such privilege all my life. I was—nervous. Shy.'

Shy was the last thing that Nabil could be described as being. He was still as naked as when she'd left him, his long, lean, golden body displayed to perfection in the sunlight streaming through the window. His jet black locks were tousled and in disarray, something that made colour rise over her skin as she was forced to remember how they had got that way, with her hands tangling in them, holding his head against her breasts. She could still feel the slide of them under her fingertips as she'd abandoned herself to the ecstasy of orgasm. Nabil was thinking of it too, or something very similar, as she saw the way his eyes darkened, a reminiscent smile curling his beautiful mouth up at the corners.

'I don't recall any—shyness,' he drawled now, his eyes mocking her openly.

'Don't claim you were thinking of me!' she flashed back.

'I was thinking of nothing else. How could I think of anything but you when you were on top of me—around me…?' His tone deepened, darkened. 'When I was inside you.'

'Nabil!' It was a fake protest, the words giving her the needed impetus to move past him, hurrying to close the door again.

'Ah yes.' There was a definite note of laughter in his voice now. 'I noticed them this time—the hordes of servants all crowding round the door.'

'There might have been someone in the corridor! And I prefer to conduct our personal business in private.'

Now that she had turned from the door, she found that she was trapped, with Nabil in front of her, effectively blocking the way between her and the rest of the room. He was so close that she could almost feel the heat of his skin, inhale the clean, musky smell of him.

'Don't you think you should put some clothes on?'

'Why?' Nabil tossed back. 'Because you're dressed now? Believe me, Zia, that is a situation I have every intention of rectifying.'

He'd caught her on the raw there somewhere. She'd actually flinched and those clear golden eyes had closed briefly as if against some spasm of pain. It had crushed any reply she had been about to make and it caught on something unexpected to see her struggling to find the words to answer him.

'Why do you have this hang-up where that name is concerned?'

But of course he knew the answer before he'd completed the question: the heir and a spare.

'It's the one my father always used. My father first,' Aziza admitted. 'The rest of the family just followed after.'

And it hadn't been shortened in affection—that much was plain.

He had never liked Farouk, Nabil admitted to himself. A hard man with cold eyes and possibly an even colder heart. A man who was always looking for what he could get out of a situation. If he could have chosen anyone else's daughter to secure the treaty and peace, then he would have done. But if he'd done that then he would have missed out on the opportunity to have Aziza in his bed—in his life. It was not something he cared to consider.

'Don't let them do this to you. You have a beautiful name. Why not use it?'

'A beautiful name—but one that should have a particular meaning. Aziza means precious—special—beautiful. To my father, I was none of those.'

And through her life she had been made to feel just the spare, the second daughter, the 'disappointment'. A fire of anger burned inside at the thought.

'I know how that works—when your parents are so invested in what you can bring—the stability of a country, the inheritance of a crown, a valuable marriage. So I make you a promise: I will always use your proper name. You will always be Aziza to me.'

He might have been aroused and excited by the

woman who had introduced herself just as Zia. But Aziza had fitted into his life as if she was the missing piece from a jigsaw.

'I chose you. And you have never been a disappointment to me.'

Something had turned a light on behind her eyes. But it was one that didn't stay. Instead it faded, drifted away again, leaving her gaze dark and clouded.

'In bed.'

'Is that not where a wife should be?'

'And to bear your children.'

'Naturally. I was thinking of my children when I chose you. You will be the mother they need.'

Was she supposed to respond to that smile? Aziza knew she couldn't find it in her to do so. Responding meant agreeing, accepting, and she needed so much more than just that. He had made it plain that he had chosen her with his senses, not with his heart. Because she turned him on and because she looked like the sort of woman who would conceive easily—carry a child to term.

'As Queen, and the mother of my heirs, I will give you the honour you deserve. Anything you want, you have only to ask.'

As the mother of his heirs.

'Anything?'

She'd ventured over the invisible line he had drawn between them and she saw his head come up, his jaw tightening.

'If you're looking for love then I don't have that to give,' he stated flatly. 'I don't have love in me. I wouldn't know it if I felt it.'

Well, that told her! Could he make things any clearer? So why did she have to keep on asking, keep on digging?

'Are you saying you don't have a heart?'

He actually laughed. But it was dark, hollow, no warmth in it at all.

'I lost my heart once. All it taught me was to use my head very carefully from then on.'

He was talking about Sharmila, of course. Her brain was stormed by those appalling images, appalling memories. The passage of time had done nothing to dilute the terrible effect they had. She had never forgotten, so how could he?

'But using my head I know that I want you. Since I met you I haven't looked at any other woman, or thought of anyone else. I want you in my life, in my bed. It's less than an hour since I was inside you and yet I'm hungry for you as if I've been starving for months.'

He made it sound as if he was paying her the greatest compliment in the world. To him, he probably was. He wanted her more than any other woman. For some that would have been enough. But was it enough to sustain her through a loveless marriage?

It would have to be. Nabil had nothing else to offer her. He had been totally open and honest about that.

And that at least was a sort of a compliment. She was desired by this man; desired by a king. It was not his fault if she wanted more. If she wanted to be loved.

But how could she ask for what he admitted he couldn't give her? If she wanted this man, she had to take him the way he was. A man with no love in him because it had been killed by that assassin's bullet as surely as if it had reached his own heart.

It was time she stopped digging and started facing up to reality. The only way to do that was to respond to him in exactly the same way as he had talked to her.

'Of course you are a king, and as such your mind must always be on your duties—to the country and the people,' she said carefully. 'The time here has distracted you, taken you away from things that need attention. I think we should return to Hazibah immediately. After all, as the King you can deal with important matters better there. And everything else…'

She let her eyes slide over him, lingering deliberately at his groin, where the black shorts had been but were now floating somewhere in the pool. If he could reduce what was between them to nothing but sex, then so could she. It would be her defence against revealing anything closer to the truth.

'It doesn't matter where we are. You can still perform your husbandly duties and I—I…'

It was as if someone had punched her in the stomach and she caught her breath sharply, needing more oxygen to carry on.

'And I can be everything you want in a wife and a queen there just as well as here.'

She would bear it, she told herself. She had to. He was giving her all that he had to give.

She would be Nabil's Queen and everything he wanted in a wife. It was her own problem if she was so needy for more than he could offer.

CHAPTER FOURTEEN

COULD SHE REALLY go through with this as she had promised herself? Aziza couldn't drive the thoughts from her head, no matter how hard she tried.

She'd told herself that this was the marriage she had expected, that she would cope with it and not ask for more. But with each day that passed it seemed that her resolve had started to fray at the edges, growing weaker minute by minute.

Nabil had given her everything he had promised her—she was at his side at all the events that demanded her presence and she could do anything she wanted with her free time. He had supported her strongly when she had set about improving the facilities for education for girls all over the country and, bypassing the official interpreters, she was the first person he called on if he needed someone to translate for him. The car he had promised her was parked outside in the palace garage, and he had even remembered how she had regretted that her father had kept her from riding after her accident and had presented her with a beautiful grey Arabian mare so that they could ride together when she exercised the animal.

Until now there was no sign of any baby on the way. While Nabil never said anything, she knew that he must watch her every month, just as the rest of the country watched her waistline when she appeared at some public event, waiting for the first sign that there was a baby on the way.

She could practically hear the sighs and groans of disappointment when it became obvious that there wasn't. As a result of her husband's—and the country's—scrutiny she had been meticulous in noting her cycle. And today, according to her diary, she was officially late. She wasn't one hundred percent certain, but perhaps this could be the first, all important sign that she had at last fulfilled her duty to her husband. Could she soon deliver the news to Nabil that she was carrying his long-awaited heir?

Maybe, when Nabil was secure in the knowledge that an heir was on the way, he would at last take the final step and have her officially crowned as his Queen?

A sudden sound at the door brought her head spinning round to see the dark, imposing figure of her husband. Surprisingly, for this time in the day, he was casually dressed, wearing a loose shirt and jeans and on his feet the boots he wore for riding. Colour flooded her cheeks; she felt sure that Nabil must be able to read her thoughts. She couldn't risk telling him until she was sure herself. Fortunately her husband seemed not to notice the fleeting guilt that must have shown in her eyes.

'Scimitar needs exercise,' he said, naming his favourite black stallion. 'And so do I. So I've come to invite you to ride with me.'

It might be weak, just giving in to her longing to be with him, but Aziza was on her feet in a moment, hurrying to change into riding gear and to head down towards the stables with him. She could take a pregnancy test tomorrow.

* * *

'Where are we going?' she asked when they were mounted and had turned their horses away from the capital, out towards the desert. A small group of body-guards followed at a very discreet distance, but they might as well have been alone. As alone as a king could be outside of his private palace apartments.

'I thought we'd head out to the oasis.'

He could only hope that the exercise, the fresh air, would ease his unsettled mood, Nabil admitted to himself. He had spent the morning trying to attend to diplomatic business but had found it impossible to focus. The recollection of just what day it was had shattered any hope of rational thought.

Ten years ago, he had started his day with everything and a future to look forward to. He had ended it with nothing. Not a hope. Not even trust.

He couldn't bear to stay in the palace and remember how it had felt to set out from there, with Sharmila on his arm, their tiny child still just a promise of life inside her growing belly. But far worse was the recollection of the return to his rooms, after the rush to hospital, the screaming siren of the ambulance. The silence of his suite had closed about him then, total and echoing, leaving him with the shattered fragments of the future lying in ashes around his feet.

He didn't intend to return to the palace, to that suite, tonight.

'We both need some relaxation, some private time away from the prying eyes at the court, with everyone watching and waiting for news.'

'You noticed?' She flushed and shifted uncomfortably, unable to quite meet his eyes.

He sought to reassure her. 'They've been watching me too,' he said wryly. 'Watching and wondering.'

He knew that the attention and the speculation was getting to her. For weeks now, she had been growing quieter and more withdrawn with each day that passed. Perhaps this break from the palace would help her relax.

'I'm sure we'll both feel better away from the pressure of expectation. Out here we can be ourselves.'

The wide smile she turned on him made him realise just how much it had been missing recently. He hadn't been able to ignore the tiny lines of concern that often formed around her beautiful eyes.

'Not the Sheikh and his Queen but man and wife.'

It was meant to reassure her but, as he said it, he realised just how much he wanted that too. He wanted to go back to the way things had been in the first days of their honeymoon. Even to the time just after the wedding day when he had come to look forward to the evenings as the best part of the day. The investigations he'd set in place had become less and less important when he'd thought of Aziza's quiet presence waiting for him.

Perhaps this way he could begin to feel that he hadn't made a terrible mistake for Aziza by choosing her to be his selected Queen. He had wanted all she represented in his memories—gentleness, warmth, understanding—for his children. And he had wanted her glorious sensuality and her luscious body in his bed for himself. But had he stopped to think whether she could handle all that went with being Queen? The lack of privacy, being the focus of all eyes, the public demands and the lack of privacy that went with the job?

She had been unprepared for the position. And he knew all about the sense of shock, of disbelief, that came with the unexpected descent of responsibility when you least expected it. He had been too young when that cloak of responsibility had landed on his shoulders, rocking his world and threatening to throw him off balance. Another reason why he'd got caught up with Sharmila. He should have known he was a damn fool where women were concerned.

No, as always, he'd thought he knew better. He'd been desperate for her company, a stupid, headstrong, lonely fool. She'd taught him that it could be better to live alone. He'd even told himself he preferred it. Now he knew different. Aziza was a calm, welcoming anchor of peace at the end of even the stormiest day.

She'd grown too; changed. The girl who had asked if it was possible to get used to being the centre of such attention now faced the crowds smiling and waving like a true queen. As a result she made it easier for him too. The attention was shared, more than halved—everyone wanted to see his new consort. She was his quiet support, his gentle strength, and when they went back to their room at night his joyous passionate lover. But he was afraid that the pressure might still break her. Had he done right to take a sweet innocent and subject her to this constant attention?

'Would you like to swim?'

The question took Aziza by surprise. All the way through the long, steady ride to the oasis, Nabil had been silent and distant, absorbed in some thoughts that he didn't let her into. She might as well not have been there at his side, the sleek elegance of her mare dwarfed by the size of his huge stallion. Although he rode easily, with a loose rein, it was always as if he was holding the powerful horse in check—or perhaps, looking at his face, it was himself that Nabil was holding in check.

So the last thing she was expecting was the casual suggestion that he tossed her way once she had slid down from the saddle, with a nod of his dark head towards the inviting coolness of the water beneath the palm trees.

'I'd love to—but I didn't bring any swimming costume.'

'That didn't worry you the last time.' A gleam of amusement lit in his eyes.

'There wasn't a party of bodyguards around then. Can't we send them back?'

'I wish.' It sounded almost as heartfelt as her own thoughts. 'But I can help you with one thing.'

Reaching into the saddle pack, he pulled out a jade coloured one-piece and tossed it her way.

'And if you have any other concerns about a place to change…'

He folded his large hand around hers and led her away from his men, rounding a huge rock to where a large, black woven tent stood at the water's edge.

It was more than a place to change, Aziza realised once Nabil led her inside. A beautifully woven carpet, glowing in rich jewel colours, covered the desert floor. Low divans piled with embroidered cushions and blankets stood at right angles to each other, each of them large enough to form a double bed.

'What are you planning?' She turned an enquiring face to Nabil.

'Not planning.' His smile flashed wider. 'It's all arranged.'

'We're staying here tonight?'

'Sleeping under the stars…' He gestured towards the roof of the tent where thousands of tiny stars were embroidered into the decorative hangings. 'And the body-guards have orders to keep their distance.'

'It will be just the two of us,' Aziza breathed, her smile widening naturally as she thought of the hours spent away from the rules and protocol of the court. As Nabil had said, just a man and a woman.

That phrase caught and stayed in her thoughts as the afternoon passed in a haze of delight. She swam in the cool, clear water of the oasis and drowsed in the warmth of the evening, sitting beside a fire to share a meal that had been brought along in the baskets slung over a packhorse's back. The firelight played over the carved planes of Nabil's face, casting shadows and light and turning those brooding, dark eyes into deep black pools.

Now Nabil took her hand again and led her towards the dark, warm privacy of the embroidered tent.

Just the two of us. Man and wife.

It was late when they finally fell into a sleep of exhaustion, tumbling into a deep, dark pit of unconsciousness which closed around Aziza, until something raw and distant, a violent, restless movement, pulled her unwillingly up towards the surface.

'*No...* No!'

It was Nabil's voice, rough and thick, his head thrashing from side to side on the pillows.

Instantly Aziza was awake, pushing herself up into a sitting position as she saw his restlessness, the way his hands flailed, as if pushing something away.

'Nabil?'

Tentatively she reached out to put a gentle hand on his arm. But it seemed that her touch only disturbed him more, making him mutter in his sleep.

'Sharmila—no.'

And that name had her freezing. Even her heart seemed to thud to a halt, her breath catching in her lungs.

Around the edge of the tent flap, she could see a thin edge of light where the dawn was breaking. For the first, the only, time, Nabil had stayed with her; he had shared her bed all night. But as a result of that she was forced to face the fact that, while in her bed, he had been dreaming of his first wife—his first—his only—love.

CHAPTER FIFTEEN

'*I LOST MY heart once. All it taught me was to use my head very carefully from then on.*'

Nabil's words came back to haunt her, making tears burn at the back of her eyes so that she had to blink hard and fast.

She had known this all the time, hadn't she? Told herself she could accept it. So why would it trouble her so much more now?

Because she could very well be carrying his child. The reality rushed at her like a tsunami. She had been able to cope with the ghost of Sharmila lingering in their marriage until now because the other woman was in Nabil's past. But now *she* could be the one carrying Nabil's heir. She could give her husband everything he wanted. Except for the one thing she wanted to share with him.

She could have his passion, throne, his child—but she could never have his love.

'Aziza?'

Nabil's voice broke into her thoughts as she saw that he was sitting up, his eyes slightly hazed, a frown drawing the black straight brows together.

'I stayed…' He sounded confused, disbelieving. 'You

are the first woman with whom I have managed to stay with the whole night since...'

He couldn't quite believe it, Nabil admitted. He had never been able to stay the night because in the depth of sleep would come the memories. The sound of the gunshot, the sting of the wound on his face, the way that the woman at his side had fallen to the ground. In the past, he had always seen Sharmila's face when he had lifted her. But these days the face he saw in his nightmares was Aziza's, and that took him down into a pit of horror from which it had been impossible to escape. The thought of being left alone again, and this time so totally alone, meant that he had had to leave the bed, walk, to rid himself of the darkness.

'You said—you spoke of your wife.'

'Sharmila.' He couldn't put any life into his voice. 'Yes, she was there.'

'I suppose it was inevitable on an anniversary like today. She must have been in your thoughts all day.'

Aziza's voice was soft, low, like a soothing balm on a barely healed wound. It was as if she knew, and truly understood, just how difficult it was to rid himself of the shadows of his past mistakes. This was what he had married her for. This was what he had seen in his memories of the young Aziza, and hoped to find in the adult woman. It was what he would have said that he wanted for his children—but right now, it was what he needed himself. The peace she brought to the darkness of his restless soul.

'You remembered?'

He took her hand, drawing it to his lips, and she reached out and touched a fingertip to the scar that marked his cheek.

'You must miss her.'

'Miss her?' His rejection was instant. 'Hell, no—'

Her start, the way that her head went back, told him that was not what she had expected. Of course, she had talked of it on the balcony, but not in the way he had wanted her to remember it.

She thought he had endured so much to keep the peace. It was true he had kept quiet about so much, hidden things away in order to ensure the uprising that had been threatening had not broken out all over again. Ankhara, the leader of the rebellion, had been such a threat, his plans carefully laid, and he had very nearly succeeded. But now he needed Aziza, if no one else, to know the real truth. He didn't want her thinking of him as some great hero when really he had been a weak, easily blinded fool.

'But you loved her.'

'Loved?' Nabil shook his head in rejection. 'I told you, I don't have that to give. Oh, I wanted her—hell, I was nineteen; my hormones were raging—I wanted her like crazy and she wanted me. Or so I believed.'

Aziza was uncomfortable with the way this was going, that was obvious. Her eyes had dropped to his hand where it held hers, to the gold band of her wedding ring, then flew back up again, to focus on his face. But something new and very different in that clear gaze scraped over his skin, making him shift uncomfortably.

'You wouldn't have liked me then, Aziza,' he told her frankly. 'I didn't like myself. I was young, foolish and totally selfish. I knew what I wanted but I didn't know what I valued. I didn't know how to find what was truly important, truly valuable. I was suddenly the King of Rhastaan, and I never wanted to be—not then, not yet. I wanted my freedom—to enjoy life. I certainly didn't want to be tied down. Married. Particularly not to a bride my father had selected for me.'

'Clementina…'

'Yes, Clementina. I wanted freedom and I cast aside a pearl of a woman as a result.'

It was only when Aziza moved to place her hand over his, to still it, that he realised he was tugging at a loose thread in the blanket, twisting it until it broke.

'And Clemmie deserved so much better than me. She deserved a man like Karim—a man of honour. I was empty, hollow. I existed only because my parents needed an heir, not because they wanted a child. I wasn't any real part of their relationship. So when I met Sharmila, and she made it plain that she was interested in me, I thought I'd found a home. But I was wrong; life soon taught me that but I didn't *know* how wrong until with you…'

'With me?' Her voice trembled on the question and her eyes were deep, dark pools of gold.

'With you I've known more peace than ever before.'

It was the truth. It was more than he had ever expected. She was his peace and he valued that peace so much that he dreaded the thought that Aziza might get caught up in Sharmila's toxic legacy. He would give the world to protect her from that. But the way that she had shifted restlessly under the covers, the way that her eyes had slid away from him, her hand pulling free from his, offered their own warning. Since she had become so restless and unsettled he had been on edge, unsure in a way he had never known before.

'What is it, Aziza?' he asked softly. 'What's wrong?'

'Wrong? It's not wrong,' she returned in a tone that somehow failed to convince. 'In fact it's just what you want—I'm pregnant,' she said baldly, but with a touch of pride that lit a flame in his heart.

She didn't sound as joyful as he might have expected, but then this was all new to her, and it came on top of everything else she had had to learn about being Queen. It didn't matter; he had enough delight for both of them.

'Pregnant,' he said, his voice thick and rough with satisfaction. 'Oh, thank heaven.'

Leaning forward, he planted a kiss on those parted lips, taking them hard and fierce with all the joy, the pride, that was in him. Now at last he really would be the King Rhastaan needed; and with Aziza at his side he could make up for all his wild and foolish days.

His doubts had been unnecessary. She would stay with him now. All right, so she would stay because of the child, not because of him, but he'd take that for now if that was what was on offer. After all, their marriage had been a political one, carefully arranged to establish the strongest treaty possible. She had little reason to stay for him, but this was enough. Better to keep her with him just for the baby than not at all.

'That is the best news ever,' he told her, taking both her hands in his and holding them tight. 'For the country— for you...'

'And for you. You must have doubted that I could give you a child.' Her voice was tight, hurt—accusing, even. 'After all, there can't be any problem with your side of things, can there? I mean, Sharmila was pregnant within weeks. You must have worried when it wasn't like that for us.'

Now what had she said? His black eyes narrowed, his mouth clamping tight over some violent curse.

'You don't want to take that as any sort of example,'

he muttered darkly. 'Sharmila was pregnant on our wedding day. With a baby that wasn't even mine.'

'What?' The shock was so great that her eyes actually blurred, unable to see his face properly, but his voice had been so strong, so bitterly sure. 'What are you saying?'

'That Sharmila's child was not mine. I thought it was—she told me it was—but the post mortem...'

He pushed both his hands through the jet darkness of his hair, ruffling it wildly.

'Sharmila was part of the conspiracy all along. She was Ankhara's niece.' His voice darkened over the name of the leader of the planned rebellion. 'They made sure I would turn away from Clementina, and then the assassination was supposed to kill me and leave Sharmila, supposedly carrying the heir to the throne, but... The whole thing went wrong.'

Aziza could find no words. There was nothing she could say. And when suddenly Nabil's clouded eyes were fixed on her face she found that all possible thought had fled from her mind. Her heart ached cruelly for the young man—scarcely more than a boy—who had found that everything he had hoped for, believed in, had been just a lie. His parents' emotional neglect had been bad enough—she knew what that felt like—but this...

All she could do was to reach for his hands, hold them, try to communicate her understanding by touch when she couldn't find the words. Nabil's eyes were just deep, black jet as they held hers in a moment of silent communication.

'I have never told anyone that before,' he stated flatly. 'Not even Clementina.'

The honour he was paying her was more than she

could ever imagine. He had kept silence over this for a decade but now he was sharing it with her.

'Wh-why me?'

Nabil's mouth quirked up at one corner into a wry, twisted smile and he spread out his hands in a gesture of resignation and surrender.

'There is no one else I could trust with it, other than my Queen.'

That word seemed to make him pause, change his mood. Throwing back the covers, he swung his legs out of the bed, lifting her to her feet and taking her with him.

'Time to get dressed, wife,' he declared. 'Time to head back to the palace—we have your coronation to arrange. I've waited too long for this. It's time you really were my Queen.'

He was heading for the doorway, throwing back the tent flap to greet the flood of bright clear daylight that swept into the tent, so he didn't see the way that Aziza's eyes, clouded and unsure, followed him, until at last she lifted her hands and rubbed them across her face, pushing away the tears of regret she was not prepared to let herself shed.

This is the best news ever... For the country—for you...

Of course the country would come first. She was surprised that he had even put her into that equation. Now, *now*, he would have her crowned as his Queen. As she had suspected, now that she had done her duty and would provide him with an heir. Until now, this hadn't mattered, but now...

Now he was forcing her to face the question that had been plaguing her for too long. Could she really bear to be his Queen, the mother of his child, and nothing more?

If only he knew that being Queen meant nothing to

her. That the only thing she truly wanted was to have his love and to be Queen of his heart.

And that was the one thing it seemed she could never be.

CHAPTER SIXTEEN

CORONATION DAY.

You could almost smell the excitement in the air, Aziza reflected, and she pushed back the covers and padded across the floor to the window. There was a buzz of electricity in the atmosphere that blew up from the streets and houses of the capital while, in the palace, already preparations must be in hand.

Rhastaan had a new queen and there was a brand new heir to the throne on the way.

No, she had that the wrong way round. Aziza closed her eyes against the wave of misery that swept through her. A brand new heir to the throne was on the way and so Rhastaan would have a new queen.

The news of her pregnancy might not yet have been announced officially, but she knew the truth. Nabil was only prepared to crown her as his Queen because she was carrying his child, so she was to get her reward in the shape of a royal crown.

No one, least of all her husband, knew just how little that reward meant to her, and how much more she would value something much simpler. The love of the man who had stolen her heart when she was only a child and had never let it go ever since.

But everything had changed. Even her sleeping arrangements had been different. Last night, the night before the coronation, Nabil had slept elsewhere, leaving her alone in their suite.

'Sleep well,' he had told her, dropping a kiss on her forehead. 'I want you to look your best for the ceremony tomorrow.'

No doubt he also wanted her to look good on the stamps, she reflected cynically, moving across the room to pick up the glorious golden gown she was to wear today. Gorgeously embroidered, resplendent with rubies and diamonds at the neckline, it should ensure that.

Slipping it on over her body, still naked from her bed, she studied her reflection in the mirror. Yes, she supposed that she looked regal enough. Soon her attendants would arrive; her hair, which was now falling wild and loose about her shoulders, would be dressed and pinned into an elaborate style. Her make-up would be done, and her hands manicured, ready to receive the ring of state that would mark her out as the Sheikha of Rhastaan.

Was she really going to go through with this? Was she really going to tie herself to a man who would never love her? A man who saw her only as a bed mate and a womb with which to breed future kings. The eyes that looked back at her as she asked herself the question looked dead, blank, as she stared out at a future that promised only emptiness.

It was far worse than when her father had set out to make her feel only the spare daughter. She wasn't even Nabil's other Queen, as she had once believed. Sharmila had shattered the young Nabil's ability to love, building on the distance and neglect of his parents to leave him a man whose heart was dead. He had spoken the absolute truth when he had told her that he had no love to give.

So was she prepared to accept that?

'No.'

She had to speak the word aloud to give it the emphasis it needed.

She was worth more than this, needed better than this. She had no doubt that her decision would cause every sort of uproar and scandal. Her reputation would be ruined, and her father would probably disown her. But one good thing to come out of this was that she no longer needed or sought her father's approval. The only thing that mattered to her was the love of the man she adored, so it was better to lose her name and her status than to lose her soul by enduring this sort of death by empty marriage. It could only turn her into someone as heart-dead as the man she had married.

She had to end this now, before it totally destroyed her. She would have to let Nabil have access to the baby of course. He was the child's father and he had every right to build his own relationship with it. Her stomach twisted at the thought of having to see the man she adored and know that he didn't love her. But she couldn't go on any other way.

A knock at the door brought her head round.

'Come in.'

The maid who came in, an envelope in her hand, sank into a deep curtsey that gave Aziza the respect due to the position she had just decided to reject.

'A letter, madam…'

Taking the envelope, Aziza saw that it was addressed in her father's handwriting. Her insides gave another cramping sensation as she wondered just what Farouk would have to say. But the arrival of the message gave her a much-needed reminder that Nabil would be preparing for the ceremony he thought was ahead of them.

She had to tell him her decision. Private hell or not, she couldn't just turn and run.

'One moment…'

A few words scribbled on a sheet of paper were all she dared communicate. She didn't want to risk the truth spreading around the palace before she'd had time to talk to Nabil.

'Take this to the King.'

The door had barely closed on the woman before she was assailed by another stab of cramp that was too disturbingly familiar to be just the effect of nerves, making her head reel in appalled realisation. Had she got this so terribly wrong? Could she really have made such a basic mistake? Why, oh, why, had she told Nabil of her suspicions before she knew for certain?

Panic clenched in her head and her heart as she headed towards the bathroom in a rush.

I need to talk to you.
The coronation cannot go ahead.

Not even a dozen short words, but Nabil had to read them over and over to try to make sense of them.

Why would Aziza send such a message *now*? Why couldn't the coronation go ahead? He had woken that morning with the hope that at last his future had opened up for him. But that was before he had received this message which seemed to bring those hopes crashing down around him once again.

Spinning on his heel, he turned and raced up the huge marble staircase, taking the steps two at a time.

'Sire… Majesty…' His chancellor's voice floated up behind him but he ignored it, racing along the corridor and slamming to a halt outside the royal suite, his heart thudding so hard that his brain would barely function.

'Aziza!'

He was shouting her name as he flung open the door, striding into the room, snatching off the white headdress and sending it flying on to a chair as he looked around him, hunting for the dark haired, slender figure of the woman who over the past six months had created the still, calm centre of his world that he needed so much.

'Aziza! Where the devil…?'

No sign of her. The bed was unmade, and the ceremonial robe she should have been wearing today was gone. But her shoes still stood in the corner, and the jewelled diadem he had sent for her to wear until the actual moment that the crown was put on her head lay at the top of the jewellery box on the dressing table.

So what had happened? Where *was* she? He checked the dressing room, the bathroom—both empty. It was as he came back into the bedroom again, frantic with worry, that the swirl of air from his robes lifted an envelope that had been lying on a chair and sent it drifting to his feet.

The writing on the address was too familiar for comfort. Any message from Farouk was potentially bad news but just what had Aziza's father found to write to her about that it had sent her running from the room? And, more important, where had she run to?

He didn't know where the inspiration came from, only that the memory connecting Aziza and her father turned his feet towards the balcony where they had first met. Avoiding the curious eyes of busy servants as he ran, he brushed away attempts to ask if he needed anything.

The only thing he needed right now was Aziza.

'Aziza!'

He stepped out on to the balcony. At first he thought that he'd got it wrong; she wasn't anywhere to be seen. But then, just as that first time, he heard a sound at the far end of it. Aziza was there, curled up on a cushioned stool, her head bent, long black hair falling down around her face, hiding it from him. But even as he watched he heard the sound again, the one that had attracted his attention in the first place. He found it impossible to interpret just what it meant. The twist of nerves in his stomach was a pain he struggled to control as he made his way towards her.

'Aziza?'

His use of her name obviously alerted her to his presence. She stilled, stiffened, but kept her head bent, those silky curtains of hair concealing any sign of her expression.

'What is it?' Nabil tried again, testing the water, trying to find out just what her mood might be. 'Was that a laugh—or are you crying?'

'Cry—oh—both…' she responded, breathy and uneven, pushing her hands beneath the fall of her hair to swipe at her cheeks before tossing back the black mane.

'Both?'

He could see now where there were faint smudges on her face where she had obviously been trying to drive away tears but, impossibly, at the same time there was still a trace of laughter in her voice, a strange brightness in her eyes. But one that had nothing at all to do with real amusement and the break in her voice made her words sound like hiccups of jerky emotion.

'What the hell…? What is wrong?'

'Oh, nothing's wrong,' she answered him airily, totally implausibly. 'Nothing for me, that is.'

It got worse. With each word her tone became more unconvincing, more unbelievable. She was hiding something and just that thought set every defensive instinct on to red alert.

'Damnation, Aziza, what the devil are you talking about? Tell me what is wrong.'

'It's Jamalia.'

She gulped in air on the words, turning each of them into a choking sob in the same moment that she picked up a sheet of paper, crumpled by the pressure of her fingers, and waved it wildly in front of her.

'This letter…'

Meeting his eyes at last, she stopped, swallowed hard, then drew in another deeper breath, forcing a more rigid control on her behaviour.

'I got a letter… From my father. It's about Jamalia.'

'And?' he prompted when the control she had managed started to slip and she clearly had to swallow hard to get a hold of herself again.

'Jamalia has run away from home—with a man. Apparently she's been seeing him for weeks, in spite of my father forbidding her to have anything to do with him. She's been more than seeing him.'

The brittle mask of composure broke, seeming to shatter into tiny pieces that scattered on to the floor at their feet as she couldn't control the brittle laughter that escaped.

'It seems that you married the wrong sister after all, Nabil.' She gabbled the words out at a ridiculous rate. 'You married because you needed an heir and chose me—because of my child-bearing hips. But, in spite of everything, I show no sign of giving you an heir while Jamalia—well, she's pregnant already.'

'But you are pregnant also. At least that's what you told me.'

His throat was so dry that he had to force the words out and they cracked in the middle, revealing the dark shadow of dread that was creeping into his soul.

'No—there you're wrong.'

Could her voice get any more high-pitched, would her control become so ruthless that her body would actually break under it? Nabil took a step forward, wanting to hold her, but she reacted as if he had made a move to strike her, eyes flaring in such a panic that he froze, feeling her rejection like a wound.

'Don't say— Aziza, *habibti*, are you all right?'

'I'm fine.'

It was so obviously a blatant lie that it had him biting down hard on his tongue, using the small physical pain to distract himself from reality.

'Fine except for cramps—period pains, and a terminal case of stupidity!' she flung at him. 'I was never actually pregnant, you see—just late. Oh, yes, I know! I *know* I should have seen a doctor—that was the obvious way to make things sure—but I thought… I didn't think, I just felt I knew.'

'And now.'

It wasn't a question. He didn't need to ask a question. It was already answered in the pallor of her face, the dark bruises of her eyes, the way that her hand rested on her body, smoothing gently as if she could wipe away the emptiness there.

'Now, nothing. I'm sorry, Nabil—more sorry than you could ever imagine. If only I had taken a test, seen a doctor before I told you, then I could have saved you all this.'

'Saved me *what*?'

'Saved you from having to organise a coronation. From—' Her voice cracked, caught up on itself and tried again. 'From having to make me your Queen.'

'I didn't have to—I wanted to. You *are* my Queen.'

Did she doubt it? Obviously she did. But how could that be when he had been unable to miss the chance of making her really his Queen and had snatched at it with greedy hands? Like her, he hadn't even thought of the need to confirm her condition because he hadn't cared. Even the suspicion of her pregnancy had given him the hope of a new beginning, the chance of making her formally his Queen and he had wanted that so much. He had wanted to show her…

'Not any more. I'm not pregnant, Nabil. I'm not carrying your heir.'

'What does that matter?' he growled. 'We can try again.'

If he had slapped her hard in the face she couldn't have looked more appalled.

'Try again?'

It was a sound of horror. One that took everything he had believed that today was about and threw it over the edge of the balcony, to shatter in the courtyard so far below.

Had he really said that? Aziza couldn't believe she had heard right. She'd been terrified that he wouldn't believe her; that the scars of Sharmila's betrayal would mean that he couldn't trust at all. She'd feared that she would meet the same reaction as she had when she had removed her veil on her wedding night and he had believed that everything was part of a conspiracy, a plot against him. Yet, now, here he was declaring cold-bloodedly that they could try again. As if all that was needed—all that mattered—was that they got busy creating another heir to the damn throne.

'I don't want to try again.'

How could she say such a thing when it was a blatant lie? Aziza asked herself. Why didn't her lips and tongue shrivel in the acid bite of the untruth she was speaking? In spite of the resolution she had made earlier, she couldn't help but long for a chance to try again—to have a hope of carrying Nabil's child, holding a tiny black-haired son or daughter close to her heart. And if there was any chance of Nabil knowing any true feeling for her then she would take that risk in a heartbeat. But there was no real love that Nabil felt. Living with that would only destroy her—so how could that be any sort of marriage to bring a baby into?

'All right.'

She had never expected such an easy response. It was impossible. Did he really care so little?

'If that is what you want.' It was flat, dead-toned. 'There doesn't need to be a child.'

'But of course there does. That was the only reason why you married me.'

'At the beginning, perhaps but—no.'

'Yes! I know why you chose me. As your Queen, I was to have your child, give the country an heir—me and my child-bearing hips.'

She ran her hands down her sides, cursed the way his gaze followed the movement. But there was something strange in his eyes, something that was so very different from the way he'd looked at her when he'd first said those words.

'But hard luck—'

Somehow she managed to put the coldness she needed into her voice and she saw his proud head go back in shocked response. She had to get this over and done with or she would weaken, risk going back on all she had resolved.

'I don't want to be your Queen. I don't want to be your wife. You can divorce me—it's easy...'

'No.' Nabil shook his head fiercely. 'No, I won't divorce you. I can't.'

'You can—you must marry someone else. Someone who can give you a child.'

'The only child I want is yours. I can't marry anyone else unless I love them.'

Was she hearing things? Aziza's head felt as if it was spinning nauseously. Had he actually used the word 'love'?

'Don't you dare talk about love,' she flung at him, desperate to bring this appalling standoff to an end. 'Not when you've already told me that you don't know what it is or how it feels. We have no marriage without that. I can't—I won't—stay without love. Our relationship is empty—dead—if I do.'

'I know.' He shocked her into silence with the force of his declaration. 'I know that our marriage would be dead without love. And it's true that I thought I couldn't feel that, didn't know what love was. But someone taught me.'

'Someone? Who?'

'You,' he said simply, taking the breath from her lungs. 'My wife...'

My wife. Not *my Queen.* Was she a fool to latch on to some sort of hope in his choice of words? But as she tried to find something to fill the silence there was a flurry of sound in the banqueting hall, and outside, below the balcony, there were cars starting to draw up, bringing guests and dignitaries to the palace for the coronation ceremony. It was time she brought this to an end and faced the life she had to live alone.

'Nabil—you have to go. As their King you have to tell them that nothing is happening today—that...'

The words faded off as he shook his head.

'I won't,' he said simply and his voice sounded strange, as if the words had cracked in the middle. 'I can't. I can't go down there and say anything to anyone as their King.'

Abruptly he moved, coming close as he had done on that first night in this same place, right here on the balcony. But in contrast to that first time, when she had felt the power and the hostility coming off him in waves, now it seemed as if he had his heart in his eyes. But did she dare to trust what she thought she read there?

'I can't do that because I can't be a king without my Queen at my side.'

Those deep black eyes held hers, and he slowly sank down on to one knee before her, making her gasp in stunned disbelief.

'Aziza—my beautiful one—you are my Queen.'

'Because...' she began but he lifted his hand, placed his fingers across her mouth to silence her.

'Don't say it. Don't ever say that I want you for the child you can bring. That might have been so at the start—when I knew I had to have a bride. I thought it was the only way. Clementina told me to find someone to make me happy but I'd given up on happiness—stopped believing in love. So an arranged marriage seemed to provide the only things I needed. But by then...'

Nabil paused, looked around at the balcony, and she knew that he was recalling that first night, their meeting in just this same place.

'By then I'd met a beautiful woman—a maid, I thought, called Zia, and she woke something in me that I hadn't known for years. Something I'd never known, if I'm honest. When the arranged marriage was planned, and I saw the two of you, I knew I could never marry your sister. Before I even recognised who you were, that night here on this balcony had stirred up memories I thought were long buried, of the first times we met. I realised then that I'd never fully been able to forget you—that you had crept into my mind and stayed there, making me measure every other female against you.'

'Nabil…' Aziza tried but he shook his head again.

'Let me say this,' he said, softly but firmly. 'Let me tell you and then—if you still want to leave—I will have to let you go. If you really don't want to be my Queen then I must set you free. But I will never be able to be the sort of king I want to be without you by my side.'

'But what if I can't have a child?' she had to ask. Had to know.

A wave of his hand dismissed the question, pushed it aside as something that no longer mattered.

'I have cousins—the throne can pass to them. I think it will have to anyway,' Nabil stunned her by declaring. 'Because the truth is that if you don't want to be my Queen, if you really want to leave, then I will have to renounce the throne. I will have to come with you.'

'You can't!' Aziza stared at him in disbelief, but if she was searching for the truth then surely it was there in those deep, dark, steadfast eyes?

'I can,' he assured her, his voice ringing with an unquestionable sincerity. 'I'd have to. Because wherever you are is where I'll be a king—with you as the Queen of my heart. But I can't be any sort of king without the woman I love in my life.'

The woman I love. Could she ask for anything more than those four simple words? Words that had no connection with a crown or a kingdom, with royalty or thrones, but only with a man and a woman and the love that they shared together. That was the crown she had looked for all her life.

She took a step towards Nabil, holding out her hand to him so that he could take it and they could go forward together from now on.

'And I can be anything—do anything—with the man I love at my side,' she declared in a voice that was strong and sure, no trace of hesitation in it.

She would have said more but he gave her no time or breathing space. Instead he rushed to his feet, gathering her up into his arms and pressing his lips against hers in a kiss that swept all her doubts, her fears, away on a burning tide of devotion. A silent, ardent declaration of how he felt in a way that was more eloquent than any words.

'My love,' he murmured against her mouth as he crushed her to him. 'My life—my wife. My only true Queen.'

* * * * *

Maisey Yates

Christmas at The Chatsfield

LUCY KENNEWICK HATED CHRISTMAS. She had for the past five years. Every single year she had spent in her husband's—soon-to-be ex-husband's—sterile mansion, void of boughs of holly, mistletoe or anything resembling a reindeer, had been bleak and soulless like the man himself.

Before her marriage to Nico she had quite liked Christmas in New York. From the beautiful department-store window displays to the glittering tree in Rockefeller Center. But after that all of the festive cheer outside had only been a reminder of the starkness inside her life.

She lifted the red skirt of her gown as she walked up the steps that led to the front entrance to the grand ballroom of the Chatsfield. This would be her first Christmas party without him since they were married, and she was determined to enjoy herself.

They had both been invited. Because when the invitations had been sent out their marriage had still been seamless, as far as the public eye was concerned.

Though, the iconic marriage of Lucy Kennewick and Nico Katsaros had never been all that it had appeared.

A marriage to shore up her failing company. A marriage of convenience.

Though, a *real* marriage. In spite of the fact they had never shared a room, never shared their personal space, they had most certainly shared a bed.

As Lucy walked into the ballroom she unbuttoned her long black coat, handing it to the man waiting to check it. As she did she became suddenly conscious of her hands, of the fact that her left hand was bare. That her ring was gone.

That her marriage was over.

She should be happy. The day after Christmas everything would be finalized, and her life would go back to normal. Her marriage to Nico would be nothing more than a blip on the radar. A starter marriage. Who in the city didn't have one of those?

She made her way deeper into the room, feeling suddenly very conscious in the bright red silk gown amid the sea of chic New York City black. The annual Christmas ball was always a can't-miss event, but since the takeover of the new CEO, interest had been heightened. So many of the people here were in attendance because they were searching for something. For a sign of weakness, for a way to ally with Spencer Chatsfield. And Lucy?

Lucy simply wanted to take this chance to start over.

But she had one thing in common with the rest of the guests. She was wearing a mask over her eyes, offering the thinnest veil of anonymity. Making her feel as though she was watching all of those around her, while keeping herself hidden from them.

Suddenly she felt a prickling sensation on the back of her neck and she lifted her head, looking into a mirror that was mounted on the wall in front of her. She could see herself, dark hair styled into loose waves, the golden mask fitted to her face, red lips, painted to match the crimson gown that formed to her slight curves, parted as if in shock.

And then she saw what had caused the prickling sensation. She had been wrong. She had been seen. Someone else was watching her. In the reflection of the mirror, her eyes connected to those of the man behind her. He was wearing a black mask, his flawless body outlined to perfection in the custom-made suit he was wearing.

Those dark eyes saw through her mask. And she saw through his.

Nico Katsaros. Her first husband. Her first lover, but never her first love. Because he didn't believe in it. And she didn't want it.

The ghost of Christmas past had come to haunt her indeed.

His wife was here. And she had the nerve to look like every Christmas present he'd been denied as a child.

Then, as now, seeing the brightly wrapped gift, all he wanted to do was to tear back the paper and reveal the treasure beneath. Then, as now, he was forbidden from doing so.

The child of a maid living in a palatial estate, he had witnessed grandeur on a massive scale from a very early age. Witnessed it, but not been allowed to partake of it.

He hated being denied. Then and now.

She was beautiful, Lucy was. She always had been. And when she had proposed a marriage of convenience between the two of them to help improve his playboy image, and to add her ailing company to his list of assets, he had been more than willing. A wife was the next logical acquisition for him, and one as beautiful as Lucy could never be a hardship.

Tonight she had outdone herself. The gown was beautiful, but he was fixated on what the pale skin beneath it looked like. He knew. He knew intimately. The silky texture, every delicate curve of her body.

He and Lucy had always been able to talk business, and they had always been able to make love.

It was everything else they found challenging.

Sex had never been an issue. He had wondered at first, because when he'd met Lucy she had seemed quite severe. All business. And yet, the way her suits had been tailored to her exquisite body had given him a hint that she was a woman who knew her appeal and also knew how to use it.

During their very short engagement they had discovered that the business arrangement was not the only perk of their union. Their attraction had been combustible from the beginning. Though, she had made him wait for their wedding night, and he had been rewarded spectacularly with her innocence and the most explosive encounter of his life.

Every encounter thereafter had only been better. And for five years, even as he felt the gulf widen between them their physical intimacy had only grown more intense.

Until she had told him she was leaving. Until she had told him it was over.

After that, all of the lust he had felt had turned into burning, brilliant hatred. As white-hot as any passion that had ever passed between them before.

Though, seeing her now, he knew that not all of the lust between them had been eradicated.

Crystal blue eyes met his in the reflection of the mirror and he began to walk toward her. The same eyes widened in horror, her lush red lips pressing into a firm line. She did not want him to talk to her. All the more reason to approach.

"Merry Christmas, *agape mou*."

Those words. Oh, dear God, those words. They had always ignited a fire in her stomach. And parts lower.

"It isn't Christmas yet, Nico." She swallowed hard, bracing herself to turn and face him, to deal with the man in the flesh rather than as a ghost reflected before her. "There are still a few hours left."

She turned, and realized too late that there was no bracing herself for impact when it came to him. Her only consolation was that the mask blunted some of his masculine beauty, the black leather concealing his strong brow and his cheekbones. But it did nothing to reduce the intensity of his dark gaze. And it certainly didn't stop her stomach from tightening painfully. Didn't stop her body from responding.

Five years she had shared his bed and nothing had taken the edge off of her desire for him.

Not even when she had grown bitter, broken over the distance that remained between them.

No matter how many times she kissed him, no matter how many times she let him inside her body, she never felt closer to him. They had sex, but they did not have intimacy. And there came a point where she could no longer bear it.

"You wouldn't know it. Based on the department-store displays, one would assume Christmas began in October."

"And yet, I would venture to say that based on our own work schedules you wouldn't know it was Christmas at all."

"What are you doing with your time these days, Lucy?"

Since you no longer have your company. The rest of the sentence remained unspoken.

She had lost Kennewick Manufacturing when she had chosen to divorce Nico. But among the many things she had learned about herself over the past few years was the fact that she now knew business couldn't fill every void. She needed more. And in order to have more, she had to escape her marriage.

"Right now? Volunteer work. I haven't decided anything about my future yet. It may surprise you to know that I'm eminently employable."

He chuckled, the dark sound rolling over her like a hit of good alcohol, warming her, making her light-headed. "That doesn't surprise me at all. You have a keen business mind, even if you are a faithless wife."

"I was never once unfaithful to you, Nico."

"Betraying your marriage vows by seeking divorce is not unfaithful?"

Lucy gritted her teeth. "Divorce is legal. I was your wife, not your prisoner."

"As the holidays have slowed things up you are still my wife."

She looked down, swallowing, or rather, trying to. Her throat was so dry she felt as though she had been snacking on cotton balls. "Yes, well, another reason to dislike this time of year."

"Perhaps you should speak to our host Spencer Chatsfield about getting a job? I'm sure the new CEO of the Chatsfield Empire would be delighted to have you. The rumor is that he is out to acquire the Harrington chain of hotels as well, so I imagine there will be more job opportunities open for those who are already in house. One would think those at the Harrington will be out of luck."

"Why would you think I'd have any interest in that?"

"Because you have a thing for powerful men, and Spencer Chatsfield is most certainly that."

Rage zipped down her spine. "Is that what you think of me? That the only way I could possibly get ahead is to use a man?"

"Your track record would suggest that as a possibility," he said, his voice hard. "However, you are wrong. It is not what I think of you. Because I do not think of you at all."

The lie burned his tongue. He thought of her. He thought of her every night as he tried to sleep. He'd thought of her when he tried to pick up a woman in a club only a few nights ago. He thought of nothing but Lucy. His body wanted no woman but Lucy.

Inconvenient, since he despised Lucy.

Their life had been comfortable, until she had left. Nothing had changed. He had not changed.

She had changed.

She had left him. And he was not done with her.

Standing there right now, looking at her in that dress, his fingers itching to tear it from her body, he *knew* he was not done with her.

The mask did nothing to dull her beauty. If anything, it added mystery.

Mystery. That was intriguing, considering the fact she had been in his bed for five years, considerably longer than any other woman in his life ever had been. And he had been faithful to her. He had not been certain he could manage that when they'd first married. But it had been easy. He'd never wanted anyone else.

Which was the issue now, considering she was no longer his wife, or rather, wouldn't be on the day after Christmas.

But he had let her walk out. He had let her do so without a fight.

He had let her get away too easy. Perhaps being married to her had made him soft. In the past no one would have dared to find Nico Katsaros in that way.

He had allowed Lucy to make him forget who he was.

And it was time that both she, and he, remembered.

"Do you know, as we have been standing here talking I find I'm remembering something," he said.

"What?" she asked.

"I am very angry with you."

"You are angry with me?" Her blue eyes flashed with rage. "You think you have the right to be angry with me?"

"Oh yes, I have every right. You made vows to me, *agape*. And you have broken them."

"Why should you care? It isn't as though you love me."

Her words hung between them, resting just below the soft strains of Christmas music that were drifting through the air.

"I do not have to love you to want you," he said.

"It would be nice if you didn't hate me."

"The sex was very hot between us when our feelings were much more bland. Imagine how good it could be now."

Her pale cheeks flushed red. "That's neither here nor there, as having sex with the man you are divorcing is hardly advisable."

"But you are wearing a mask. As am I. We could be anyone."

"But we are not," she said, her breasts rising on a sharp breath.

"So serious, Lucy," he said. "Always. Much too serious."

"Life is serious. You have never seemed to take it that way."

"Obviously you don't know me very well, Lucy."

Furious blue eyes met his. "Whose fault is that?"

"It doesn't matter. Not if we are strangers."

He let the words simmer there for a moment.

The fire in her eyes chilled, crystallized. "What exactly are you proposing?"

"That we leave the past here. And go upstairs and have one last night together. One last Christmas. You look every inch like a present just for me, and I find I cannot wait to unwrap you."

Lucy could only stare at her husband, stunned.

Nico was holding out forbidden fruit, and she desperately wanted to grab hold of it. To do more than simply take a bite. To seize it, to savor it.

But even as she battled her desire to speak the *yes* that hovered on her lips, her insides curled in on themselves, retreating as though they'd been touched by fire.

Because she remembered why she'd asked for the divorce in the first place. Because she remembered that sex—no matter how good—couldn't replace real, emotional intimacy. That it wouldn't fill the emptiness in her, or fix the loneliness that always hit her with the force of a hurricane after they finished making love and Nico went back to his own bedroom.

Which meant that no matter how intensely her body

burned, she could not submit herself to that kind of pain. Not again.

"This *present* is no longer for you."

His dark eyes burned into hers. "Is that so? Is someone else going to open you up this year, *agape*?"

"Perhaps," she lied.

"Then you must point him out to me," Nico said, his tone hard.

"For what purpose?"

"So that I can kill him."

A strange little zip of pleasure wound its way through her body. Nico was passionate about business, he was passionate in the bedroom, but in his verbal exchanges with her he had never been anything but measured, calm. Disinterested almost. He had certainly never expressed jealousy. And that was what this was, jealousy. Her soon-to-be ex-husband was jealous. Of a fictional man who didn't exist anywhere outside of a tiny little implied falsehood.

"You're *not* going to kill my lover," she said, unable to resist pushing him a little bit further.

"You think not? But then you must ask yourself, Lucy, if you ever knew me."

"If I didn't know you, whose fault was it? Mine or yours, Nico?"

"Perhaps it is both of ours."

She sucked in a sharp breath. "Do you think so? I never kept anything from you."

He reached out, taking hold of her chin to study her face, forcing her eyes to meet his. "Did you not?" His gaze was intense, focused. He slid his thumb along her bottom lip, sending sparks of pleasure along her spine. "I very much believe that you kept secrets from me."

Every guilty word she had left unspoken between

them built up inside her chest. "I can't fathom you would have ever cared to hear my secrets."

"So instead you will tell them to another man?"

"What will I get in return if I tell them to you?"

"Pleasure. Have I ever denied you pleasure?"

"No." She blinked hard. "But in the end it wasn't enough."

"For a marriage, perhaps. But for a night?"

She cleared her throat. "Even if I did intend to sleep with another man, you would try to seduce me away from him?"

"If in fact you do intend to sleep with another man tonight, then I am certainly angry with you. But not angry enough to cut off my nose to spite my face, so to speak. And anyway, I would rather have you in my bed than know you were in bed with someone else."

"And what about you? Going back to the legions of women you used to have before you married me?"

"There has been no one else. I want no one else," he said, his voice rough.

"Really?" His words soothed the wound she hadn't been aware was there.

"But it was not the same for you?"

"Of course there is no one else. There was no one before you. Why would I find another lover so quickly after you?"

A slow, satisfied smile spread over his features. And she knew she had made a mistake. Knew that she had forgotten she was talking to a predator. One who saw her as prey.

"Perhaps I should not be so gratified to hear this, but I am."

"That does not mean I'm going to sleep with you."

"All right," he said, his tone measured, calm. She

wasn't fooled. "But if you will not sleep with me, perhaps you would consider dancing with me?"

Nico's heart was pounding in his head, the metallic tang of anger only just now receding from his tongue. It had been a lie, and he was grateful for it. She was still his wife, after all, even if it was for only one more day.

After that, once she was no longer his, she could have whomever she wanted. But until then, she belonged to him. If she was spending the night in anyone's bed in these last remaining hours of their marriage, it would be his.

"Dance with me," he repeated.

"Just a dance?"

"If you wish."

He extended his hand, his chest tightening as he evaluated the expression on her face, partially concealed by the golden mask. There was fear in her eyes, trepidation. He had not seen her look at him that way since their wedding night. When she had been a virgin. When she had been filled with uncertainty as to what would pass between them. He had taught her, and quickly, that there was nothing to fear from him, not the marriage bed. And while they had never trusted each other with everything, they had trusted each other physically. He could see that he had lost that during their six months of separation.

But then, she intended to separate from him forever, so perhaps that should not come as a surprise.

"One dance," he said, unable to remain patient. Unable to wait for her to make the next move.

"One." She curled her delicate fingers around his and he fought the urge to cling to her tightly, to tug her against his chest and kiss her now, to prove to her that whatever she believed, whatever she pretended, whatever those signed divorce papers waiting to be filed said, her body still belonged to him.

He resisted, but only just, playing the part of gentleman as he led her out to the dance floor. Everything in him longed to pull her tight against him, and yet he managed to draw her into a respectful closed hold.

Oh yes, he was very much playing the part of the gentleman he'd never been.

The better to lure you into bed, my dear.

She looked up at him, blue eyes wide, as though she had heard the thought. He said nothing, only raising an eyebrow in response.

He was unbearably conscious of the feel of her skin beneath his. And of the fact her hand seemed different somehow.

Her ring. Her ring was gone.

"You have taken off my ring?" he asked.

"Yes. We're divorcing." She looked down and he knew then she'd caught sight of the gold band he still wore on his left hand. "You still wear yours?"

"I was not the one who asked for a divorce," he said, his tone closing the subject neatly.

He didn't want to discuss why he still wore the sign of their commitment, not when he couldn't even explain it to himself.

She looked away and he could see a pulse beating at the base of her throat. He wanted to press his lips to the delicate skin there, feel for himself the effect he was having on her.

It was so rare for him to touch her outside the bedroom. After they'd established themselves as a couple, they had never bothered with such shows of romance. Why would they? Their marriage had never been about that.

Now though…now that he was staring into forever without her, now that he was looking at her, watching her body sway to the music, seeing her dress swirl around her feet, around his legs, a bright shock of crimson against the black suit pants, he regretted it.

He released his hold on her hand, tracing a line down her cheek, meeting her eyes. "How long has it been since we danced?"

Lucy looked away from Nico, trying to get a hold on her senses. They were currently galloping ahead of her like wild horses, her heartbeat keeping time with imaginary hoofbeats. How had she allowed herself to forget the effect he had on her?

She should have known that the moment he touched her she would be lost.

It had been that way from the beginning.

She remembered clearly just before they had announced their engagement how he had demanded they test their chemistry. He was not, he had said, marrying a woman whose bed he had no desire to be in. She had been angry then. Because in her mind passion had nothing to do with their arrangement. For all she cared, he could take mistresses.

At least, that had been her feeling just before his lips had touched hers.

From that moment she had known she would be his, and his alone. And that she would demand he be hers. That kiss had changed something in her, had opened up a well of deep longing she hadn't realized was there. He had made her aware in that moment of how much of life she had been missing pouring herself into her work at the exclusion of all else. Doing her very best to continue on the legacy her father hadn't been able to see through.

After his death when Lucy was nineteen, she had become obsessed with the idea of keeping things going. Of taking the company to the place her father had imagined it could go. But somewhere in all of that, in the midst of trying to live out someone else's dreams, she had lost pieces of herself. Had become hollow, incomplete. And Nico... Teaching her to want again... He had made her so painfully aware of it.

From there, it had been a slow descent into madness. Of becoming increasingly aware of that emptiness until she'd had to change something. Ironically, without Nico she never would have realized the emptiness was there. Ironic, because it was her feelings for him that made her so aware, that made it impossible to stay.

That made it so painful to leave.

Yes, she had told him in the beginning she had no need of love.

She had been a fool.

Because the moment his lips had touched hers five long years ago, she had realized that everything she believed about herself was a lie.

And on her wedding night she had discovered that not only did she desperately want love, craved it, but she wanted it from her husband.

The man who had vowed to stay with her in sickness and in health, for richer or poorer.

The man who had also vowed, after the wedding ceremony, once they were alone, that he would never, ever love her.

Memories of the past echoed through Nico as he twirled his wife around the dance floor. Strange that an action so foreign to them should conjure up memories. More than memories, there was a strange, hollow ache. Of memories that should have been.

He had not taken her dancing. They had danced at their wedding, as they had been expected to do. Once at a gala when they had been establishing their couple status with the public. But never since.

Regret lanced him, stealing his breath. This would be the last time they danced. He had not appreciated that before. Had not fully appreciated all of the things he would never do again with her once they had divorced.

Certainly, there would be other women. Of course there would be. He had not been a monk prior to his marriage, so it stood to reason he would not be after. And yet, the prospect did not fill him with excitement. Not in the least. He did not feel as if he had been un-chained from a shackle. Rather, he felt as though he were walking back into a dungeon he had already been freed from once.

A strange feeling. Ridiculous.

And yet, he could not shake it off. Not now he had had it.

He tried to remember the last time they had made love. He had not been conscious of the fact it would be the last time. Her request for a divorce had come out of the blue, during the middle of the day. There had been no opportunity to say goodbye. No opportunity to ce-ment the end of their relationship with a final coupling.

He could no longer let that stand. He could not en-dure it.

This was to be their last dance. And tonight, Christ-mas Eve, would be their last night together.

Nico Katsaros was a man who went after what he wanted. And right now he wanted to seduce his wife.

"Good thing we have the masks. We might have caused some gossip otherwise," Lucy said, her voice soft.

"Would that be the worst thing?"

"There would be no truth to the rumors."

"Is there no truth in this?" he asked, taking the opportunity to trace the lush outline of her ruby lips again, her warmth and softness beneath his fingertip a tease he could scarcely withstand.

"Attraction. But we've been down that road. It ends. I ended it."

"It does not end for two more nights. Tonight. We can have tonight."

"Nico…"

And suddenly, he was not content to simply touch her lips. He had to taste them as well.

With the music in the background promising with sincerity that the singer would be home for Christmas, Nico bent his head and kissed his wife.

And for the first time in six months, he did indeed feel as though he was home.

Surely, over the course of five years of marriage, Nico had kissed her thousands of times. But in this moment she forgot them all. She forgot everything but this. But his lips on hers, in this moment. Forgot everything except what a revelation this was.

She clung to him, curling her fingers around the collar of his suit jacket, holding him to her, afraid that this moment, this man, would disappear back into the ether if she let go for more than one second.

It was ridiculous to want to hang on, when she was the one who had decided they needed to let go. And yet, here she was. Hanging on to him as though he were the only thing keeping her afloat in the storm.

Don't do this to yourself again.

Her heart was screaming at her. Six months. She had spent six months trying to get over Nico Katsaros and now she was going to fall willingly back into his arms? Back into his bed? She knew how this would go. There was no twist ending awaiting her.

But she couldn't resist. She never could. No, not from that first kiss all the way until this one. She had never been able to resist.

"One last time," he said against her mouth, his voice rough. "Give me this. Please."

"Why?" she whispered.

"So that I know it is the last time."

"What do you mean?"

"You surprised me with the divorce. I am certain that you knew the last time we made love would be the last time. But I did not."

Her face heated. Because she did know. She had been so acutely aware that she was saying goodbye to him the night before he left for that last business trip. She had known that she would be giving him the divorce papers when he returned. But he had no way of knowing that. She had known that last night that it was goodbye. And she had said it, with her body. Carried it with her even now.

"I didn't think you would care." She hadn't thought he would. Not for one second. She was surprised he hadn't replaced her in his bed already. She had never imagined she was special. She was just convenient.

"I care very much. And I am owed my goodbye."

She tried to squash the little bit of hope blooming in her chest. He cared about sex. He didn't care about her. His pride was likely wounded by her abandonment. Unsurprising, considering Nico was a very proud man.

And she wasn't nearly proud enough. Right now she felt needy, weak. Desperate for one more time.

"Then I'll give it to you. One last night."

He nodded once, his expression like stone. "One last night."

He broke their hold, his hand wrapping around hers as he led her from the dance floor. Every eye was on the masked couple as they broke through the crowd, moving quickly toward the lobby of the hotel.

Her heart was in her throat as they approached the front desk, and then, off to the left, she spotted a man in a suit. Tall, arresting.

Spencer Chatsfield.

Nico paused, then redirected their movements. "Hello, Mr. Chatsfield. We need a room for the night. Give us the best you have."

Spencer arched a brow, assessing them both, his expression carefully neutral. "Of course."

The moment Nico and Lucy were inside the elevator, the doors closed. Nico turned to her, pinning her against the wall, his hands on either side of her head. Restraint be damned. He had been nothing but patient. Nothing but restrained in the months since she had served him with divorce papers. Hadn't he given her everything she had demanded? Certainly, he had punished her by withholding her company from her, but she had broken her vows, and it was no less than she deserved.

Anger was once again penetrating the fog of lust that had descended over him. For a long time now, there had been only anger, blinding, white-hot anger. And now there was both. An intense need that was threatening to choke the life out of him combined with a kind of futile rage that he imagined one felt when they were watching the life's blood drain out of something precious. A kind of rage directed at the universe, a rage that had no recourse, no productivity. A rage that could fix nothing. A rage that could do nothing but simply be, filling up his entire being until he was driven by it, consumed by it.

He felt helpless in the face of it, and so, he dipped his head and consumed her. Poured all of it onto the woman who had caused it.

He broke the kiss, his lips still touching hers. "You have never done what I expected. You have never done what I asked."

She looked at him, glittering blue eyes filled with an anger that matched his own. "How can you say that? I was nothing but the perfect wife to you."

"You left me. And before that you tempted me. That was never a part of our bargain."

"I never tempted you. Temptation implies that it was something you wanted to resist. You demanded that I prove we have chemistry. And once we were married I was your business partner during the day and your whore at night. Nothing more. Never anything more. Don't you dare try and pretend I surprised you somehow. All I ever wanted was the business end of the arrangement. I never wanted this."

"You never wanted my kiss?"

"I never wanted to *need* it."

"And do you need it? Have you spent nights as I have? Aching, alone, desperate for something you know you can only have with the one person you can never touch again?"

She looked down. "I don't—"

He gripped her chin and forced her to look up at him. "Speak to me. Not to the floor."

"Yes," she said.

"I promise you one thing. After tonight you will burn for me forever."

By the time she and Nico entered the hotel room, she was shaking. His words were echoing in her mind.

After tonight you will burn for me forever.

She feared it was true. Because if the past few months were any indicator, she would never forget what it was like to be touched by him, kissed by him. She had a feeling that even if she went forward with life, filling up those empty spaces as best she could, there would always be one left vacant. Hollow. A space that could only ever be filled by Nico.

Nico sat on the edge of the mattress, leaning back, his thighs spread, the outline of his arousal clearly visible through his dark dress pants. Yes, she wanted him. Yes, she was going to have this. Even if it did make her burn. Forever and ever after. It would be worth it.

Just have him look at her like this again. To have him touch her again.

She reached up, ready to untie the mask that concealed part of her face.

"Leave it," he said, his words clipped, hard.

She lowered her hands. "And are you leaving yours?" she asked, looking at the slash of black leather still resting over his eyes.

"There is a certain appeal to it, don't you think? The opportunity to come together as strangers again. Perhaps we will learn new things, rather than simply assuming we already know them?"

She clung to part of his words, held them close to her

chest. Strangers. Maybe if she could think of him as a stranger, this wouldn't hurt quite so much. Maybe she could get what she wanted from this without the pain.

She grabbed hold of the zipper tab on her dress, and slowly began to lower it. Letting her gown fall loose, leaving her standing there bare before her husband.

Nico took in the sight of his wife's body, her every delicious curve bared for his inspection. Only two things remained. Black panties that scarcely concealed anything, rather framing the part of herself he was most interested in. And the mask, a brilliant gold against her skin. His gift, unwrapped in all her glory.

Dark curls cascaded over her shoulders, her lips a crimson temptation.

He recalled the first time he had seen his wife, in her prim little business suits. He could never have imagined they would end up here. About to make love in a hotel room, wearing masks. On the brink of divorce.

He had a moment of feeling as though he were in someone else's life. A life not his own.

He'd had this woman. His wife. And he had somehow let her escape. Nico Katsaros, who failed at nothing. Who had dragged himself up from the bottom rung of society to the very top. And yet, it had not been enough. It had not been enough to keep his wife with him.

Had he not offered her everything? Money, security for her business, sex.

Somehow, as far as this woman was concerned, he was still not enough. He hated that feeling. Loathed it more than anything else on earth. He had spent all of his life being treated as though he was not enough, as though he was deficient because of his birth.

She had no right to treat him that way. Not now. No one did. He owned the world.

But you do not own her.

He gritted his teeth against that reminder. Perhaps not. Not in the grand scheme of things. But tonight he did.

"Come to me, Lucy. Give yourself to me," he said, each word a struggle.

She obeyed, moving nearer to him, pressing her knee into the mattress beside his thigh. "I thought we were strangers tonight?"

"If you please." He ran his thumb along the edge of her mask, then stretched up to kiss her mouth. "Show me what you like."

Lucy was shaking, her hands aching to touch, her body hollow with the need to be possessed by him. It was terrifying to need like this. This was why she had consented to marry Nico in the first place to save her father's ailing company. Because as far as she was concerned, a convenient marriage was the safest route to take. She didn't want to love, not again.

Everyone in her life she had loved, she had lost. Her mother had left before she was born, her father died far too soon…

She had never wanted to submit herself to that kind of pain again. That risk of loss.

It was why there had been no other men before Nico. She had avoided relationships, avoided attachments. She had imagined it would be easy to steer clear of emotional strings with a man like Nico. A man whose foundation was set upon business, his personal life built upon the sand, ever shifting and reshaping. He'd had a reputation as quite the playboy prior to their marriage.

The sort of man women linked themselves to for an evening, but no more.

Foolish girl she had been, she had figured she would simply do the same. Connect herself physically with no emotional repercussions.

But she had been wrong. So very wrong.

He was right—she was keeping secrets from him. But it hadn't started that way.

Something had changed in her over the course of their marriage, taking root in her soul. Building, growing, until it had been almost impossible to hold back anymore. She had tried to deny it, not even allowing herself to think the words.

But they were there. Echoing through her all the same.

And as Nico rested his hand on her hip, dark eyes intent on her, she let them flow through her for the first time. Let her mind form them fully.

She had her secrets. But they were not the sorts of secrets he imagined.

Her deepest secret was that she had fallen in love with her husband.

Nico was thankful they were wearing the masks. Otherwise, he knew Lucy would be able to see the raw hunger on his face. Would be able to see just how close he was to losing control.

He moved his palm up from her hip, along the elegant curve of her waist, to the full, brilliant temptation of her breasts. A mere mask could never make them strangers, though he appreciated the small barrier it provided. Still, had he been wearing a blindfold he would've known it was her. Would have known the particular softness of her skin, the exact slope of the indent of her waist, just where her breasts grew fuller.

He knew her body as well as he knew his own.

This was the last time.

That was the agreement.

Her hands went to his tie, delicate fingers slipping the silk through the knot. He had forgotten the simple pleasure of having her undress him. The beauty in anticipating their coming together. Before their marriage he had been with countless women, but from the moment his lips had touched hers, he had never wanted another.

Slowly, she slipped her fingertips inside his shirt, her palm resting over his raging heartbeat.

He lifted his gaze from her beautiful body to her eyes. She was trying to hide too. Trying to use the mask to conceal how she felt in the intensity of this moment. He raised his own hand, placed it over hers, trapping it against his skin. Then he closed the distance between them and kissed her.

Lucy made quick work of her husband's clothes, repeating actions she had carried out hundreds of times before. But this was different. Final. It made her ache.

She drank in the sight of him. His broad shoulders and chest, sprinkled with just the right amount of chest hair. His well-defined abs that shifted and rippled with each indrawn breath. And of course, the most male part of him, the part of him that she was desperate for now.

She memorized every detail. The flex of his thighs, the way his fingers curled around the bedspread, the gold wedding band he still wore bright against his dark skin, the tendons in the backs of his hands standing out as he fought to anchor himself to the bed.

She straddled his lap, kissing him deeply as she

pressed her breasts against him. It was sexual, there was no denying it, but there was also something deeply emotional about being close to him like this again. Being skin to skin.

She had, after years of it, taken such intimacy for granted. Had been certain it hadn't been intimacy at all. But now that she had been living without him, she knew that hadn't been true. Recognized that there had been more emotion when they'd touched than she had begun to imagine. Empty, she had allowed herself to believe it was empty.

Now she felt that evaluation may have been unfair.

"Have you continued to take your contraceptive pill?" he asked, his voice rough, strained.

He was as near the edge as she was, and she found it immensely gratifying.

She nodded, because speech was beyond. His mouth went slightly slack, abject relief visible on his face even with some of his features obscured by the mask.

He wrapped his arm around her waist, moving his hand down to cup her rear, and at the same time sweeping her panties to the side. She shifted her position, and allowed him to slide deep inside of her.

Tears stung the backs of her eyes, and she shut them tight to try to keep them back.

How had she ever thought this was empty?

This was the last time. And she feared that without Nico, she would never be anything but empty ever again.

He was surrounded by her, lost in her. The feel of her, the scent of her. He reached up, sifting his fingers through her silky curtain of dark curls, relishing the sensation. He flexed his hips, sliding deeper inside the damp heat of her body.

He had thought their first time, five years ago, was powerful. But it was nothing in comparison to this. Because in their first time had been the promise of forever, while this was the promise of an end. And with that came the desperation to make it count, to make it last. To make sure she would burn, forever.

Because he would.

He grabbed hold of her bottom, moving into a standing position, wrapping her legs around his waist, keeping himself buried deep inside of her. He turned and lowered her back to the bed, reversing their positions and thrusting down inside of her.

He was as deep in her as he could possibly get, and it wasn't enough. It would never be enough.

She gasped, arching against him, and he captured the sound with his mouth, kissing her as he allowed himself to get lost in the rhythm of their bodies. Lost in her.

Soon, too soon, his climax rushed up to meet him, overtaking him like a savage beast, grabbing him by the throat and shaking him hard, leaving pleasure to bleed out through his body in an unstoppable tide. He gritted his teeth and thrust into her one last time, grinding against the bundle of nerves at the apex of her thighs, holding position until she made the sweet familiar sound of release, her internal muscles tightening around him.

He didn't move, not for a long while. Her red lips parted, a long sigh escaping.

And then a single tear tracked from beneath her golden mask and slid down her cheek, leaving a dark blot on the pillowcase.

"Lucy?" he asked, moving away from her.

She shook her head. "No. No names. Please. Please let's be strangers."

* * *

Lucy was gasping for breath, a haze of pleasure tangling with the sharp, keen clarity of what she had just done. Of the fact that it was over.

He started to get up, as was his routine after they made love. For all five years of their marriage, they would make love and he would leave, go back to his own room, leave her there with nothing more than his scent on her pillow to keep her company as her sheets cooled.

She couldn't stand that right now. Just this once, she needed him to stay.

"Don't go."

He paused. "But you're upset."

"No. Yes," she said, laughing slightly while she wiped the moisture from her cheeks. "I don't know what I am. But I don't want to be alone."

"You like to be left alone. After we…"

"What made you think that?"

"You prize your space, Lucy. I have always tried to respect that. You made it very plain when we were first married that you wanted to sleep alone."

His words hit her like a brick. They weren't wrong. She had made a very big deal about wanting to preserve her space. But that was before they were married. Certainly before they had shared years of intimacy. Surely, he must have known that she would want him to stay.

"I didn't always want space," she said.

"When? When did it change?"

She knew when. But she didn't want to tell him.

"We were strangers when we first married. Of course, after we got to know each other. After it was more than just physical… I suppose I never told you."

"No."

"I wished you would stay." So much easier to tell him

these things while she was wearing the mask. While she was pretending they were just strangers, talking. Yes, they were talking about a shared past, but somehow the game, the idea, allowed her the distance she needed to speak to him without falling apart.

"I would have liked that," he said, his voice rough.

"We kept too many secrets."

Dark eyes met hers, and he moved nearer to her again. "Did we? What were yours? Tell me your secrets, *agape*."

Nico watched the pulse beat hard at the base of her neck, watched as the delicate color leached from her cheeks. She was so beautiful. He had always thought so. But he didn't know if he had ever *felt* it.

He felt it now. Echoing in his soul, reverberating down deep in his bones. The kind of beauty you didn't just witness, but the kind that took up residence inside you. Changed you. How had he been blind to it until he had lost it?

"You don't want to know about me," she said, her voice soft.

"There will never be another chance for me to learn. And we are just strangers. So tell me. Tell me who you are. Then, when we leave here, perhaps we will not be strangers. Though, we will not meet again," he said.

"You know everything there is to know about me."

"No, I don't. Because we are strangers. Talk to me like I am a stranger, and not your husband. And I daresay I will learn more in that conversation than any we have had in the past five years." He didn't know why he was making the demand, didn't know why it suddenly seemed so important. Only that it did.

She shifted her position, rolling to her side, and he

watched her breasts move with her. Completely captivated, but not only by her body—by the words she would speak next. "All right. You know my mother left. And that it was just me and my father. And I wanted… I wanted so badly to please him. And I did. I poured everything that I was into learning about Kennewick, into helping him with ideas. I wanted to be involved in it so that we would have something in common. And he loved sharing all of that with me. And then he died. And Kennewick was all I had. By the time you and I met… I felt as though everything that I had ever cared about I was destined to lose. So that's why I couldn't find someone to be my maid of honor at the wedding. And that's why there were no men before you. Because earning the love of the only family member I had left meant pouring everything into the company. And I did love Kennewick. But you can love a business, and you can love the money it brings in. But it can never love you back." She took a deep breath. "Finally, I realized that. I realized that no amount of pouring into it would replicate the love I had lost when my father died. And so, I decided I was tired of pouring in and getting nothing back. I decided I was tired of being empty."

"You felt… Empty? Even when you were with me?"

She lifted a bare shoulder. "Sometimes being skin to skin with someone and knowing they don't care for you is even more devastating than simply being alone." She pushed herself into a sitting position, drawing her knees up to her chest. "Now…tell me your secrets."

Lucy watched, waited to see if he would turn away from her, or if he would share. She wanted him to tell her, wanted to tear down that wall that he kept between himself and the world, himself and her, and finally understand the man she had shared her life with for half a decade. Of course, it wasn't fair. Because she had talked of familial love, and manufacturing companies, and never once spoken of the fact that what had truly left her feeling empty was loving him when she knew he didn't love her back.

"I was the bastard son of a poor woman. I worked hard, got straight A's in school, got scholarships, worked my way from the ground up at one of the largest national conglomerates… But you can find all this out by reading my bio."

"But we are sharing. As though we're strangers," she said. "What inspired you to work hard? What inspired you to change?"

There was a slight pause. "I saw opulence all around me every day, and yet I was not allowed to partake in it. I vowed that I would have my own piece of that opulence someday. I was so tired of being denied."

It was easy then, to imagine him as a small boy, surrounded by the luxuries of the world while constantly being told they were off-limits. How confusing it must have been.

"You must be proud. Of everything you have achieved."

"Typically. Typically, I am. And yet, I find myself being denied again. I don't like it, Lucy. I don't like it one bit."

"What have you been denied?"

His dark eyes blazed into hers. "You."

Her heart leaped against her breastbone. "Find another wife. It won't be difficult for you."

"But it's you that I want. I want you."

"Why? Because I matter? Because you're still a small boy throwing a tantrum over the things you can't have?"

A feral growl escaped his lips, and she found herself pinned against the mattress, Nico above her, his expression fierce. And for the first time that night, he reached up and tore off the mask.

"Am I a boy? I think not. Perhaps you need me to show you again that I am in fact very much a man."

"Why would you need to show me?" she asked, desperation pouring through her. "Why should you care?"

"Do not forget that you are the one who demanded to divorce, *agape*. Not me. I did not want this. I never wanted it."

"Why?" she asked, ferocity lacing her tone. "You haven't given me a satisfactory answer to my question."

He growled, flexing his hips, giving her a taste of his growing arousal, and in spite of herself, her body responded. "Is this not answer enough?"

"No. You have always acted like it should be enough. It isn't enough."

"Why not? I gave you my name. I gave you my money. I saved your failing business. I gave you my home. A place in my bed. And you reject me. You tell me I'm not enough. I made vows to you, and still I am not enough."

"Because you didn't give me what I wanted."

"You have never told me what you wanted," he said, desperation filling his tone now, matching her own. "You didn't tell me you wanted to share my bed all night. You didn't tell me you wanted to share a room. You kept these things from me, and then you punished me for not guessing what you never spoke out loud."

There was no response she could give to that. Because he was right. She had never told him what she wanted. Had never told him what she felt, that she was empty, that she was desperate for more from him. She hadn't told him that she loved him. She had been consumed with protecting herself, with preventing another loss. So she had run, not realizing the fatal flaw in her plan. She already loved him, so whether or not she told him, whether or not she ever gave him the chance to reject her, she would lose him if she ran.

But she didn't know if she was brave enough to stay. Didn't know if she was brave enough to speak those words to him, to watch his face change. To one of horror, of pity. He didn't want love; he had stated it plainly. Had told her explicitly after their wedding that theirs would never be a union held together by emotion.

So she had believed him.

What you wanted changed. Perhaps what he wanted has changed too. But you will never know, because you are a coward.

It was true. She was.

And it had to stop.

She curled her fingers around her mask and pulled it away. And they were Nico and Lucy again. There was no more hiding. She refused to hide anymore.

"I still haven't told you my last secret."

Nico looked down at his wife, her eyes glittering with emotion, and he felt his rage drain away. He moved away from her, pushing himself into a sitting position and forking his fingers through his hair. "I'm sorry, Lucy."

He heard the rustle of the covers as she sat up, felt the light touch of her fingertips against his shoulder. "Do you want to hear my secret?"

His chest seized up tight. "Is it fair to say that I'm not sure?"

"I suppose so. Since I'm not sure I want to tell it. But I realized that all of the silence between us is what broke things. So I doubt there's anything I could say now that would make it worse."

"We are getting divorced the day after tomorrow. It doesn't get worse than that."

She laughed softly, her breath fanning over his bare skin. "I suppose so." Still, she said nothing. She only moved nearer to him, pressed her body against him, holding him.

"You're stalling, *agape*."

"You always call me that," she said, her voice soft.

"I suppose I do."

"From the beginning. You've always called me that."

Discomfort crawled over his skin. "Yes. It is a common endearment."

"It means *love*."

"I'm well aware of the meaning."

"I used to find it slightly annoying. I mean at first. Because it was all a charade, and neither you nor I were pretending to have any finer feelings. But one day…one day you said it and everything sort of slowed down. And I realized that whether or not you meant anything when you called me that it meant something to me. Because, Nico, I love you."

Heat and cold rushed through Nico's body, a reaction he could not have anticipated.

But then, his wife's words were nothing he could have ever anticipated. She loved him? And she was telling him this two nights before their divorce was final.

He turned to look at the clock. After midnight. Not even two nights until their divorce was final. It was Christmas now.

He stood, collecting his clothes and putting them on

as quickly as possible. He was aware of Lucy watching him, but he didn't look at her. He couldn't look at her. He was too lost in the feelings riding through him. Anger. Pain. But most of all, fear.

It was the fear that won.

"Our last night together has come to an end," he said, keeping his eyes fixed on a place on the wall behind her. "Merry Christmas, Lucy."

And then he turned and walked out the door.

It was a truly vile Christmas, thank you very much. No matter how resolutely the radio played music proclaiming it a merry one, Lucy simply couldn't feel it.

She had done it. She had told him. Confessed all, and he had rejected her. No, he had not even had the decency to reject her. He had simply walked out. With nary anything but a season's greeting.

She should feel vindicated. Obviously, she had been right asking for the divorce. Obviously, no amount, or lack, of communication could have possibly altered the course of their relationship. She had changed, what she wanted had changed, but what he wanted hadn't.

Certainly, he had been more than willing to have sex with her, but that was no indication of any finer feelings. Typical.

She took a sip of wine, then set her glass back down on the sideboard in the living room. The crystal made contact with the wood surface with a resounding click, echoing against the walls of her family home. Highlighting the fact that she was truly alone.

Here she was, living the exact thing she had been afraid of. Loving again. Losing it again.

The only positive thing she could say was that she was living. For now, she would take it.

The doorbell rang, and she crossed the expansive living area, heading toward the entry. If it was carolers, she could not promise she wouldn't throw them in a snowbank. She wasn't feeling particularly cheered, and she didn't really want anyone to try.

She paused at the door and looked through the security glass. And then her heart stopped. There were no Dickensian street urchins, no carolers of any kind.

It was Nico.

She opened the door to the town house, her sadness suddenly washed away by a torrent of anger. "What do you want? You didn't hurt me enough last night? Have you also come to step on my toe? Get a red wine stain on the cream-colored rug? Or perhaps something else similarly damaging?"

"No," he said, his voice ragged. For the first time, she paused and looked at him, really looked. And she noticed he appeared as though he had not slept since he had left her in the hotel room. "I came here because I have one more secret to tell you."

The last time Nico had felt so nervous, he had knocked over a vase in the hallowed halls of the home his mother had worked in. He had known then, though he had been only a child, that he had broken something priceless. That there would be no fixing it. That the only way out would be if those he had wronged forgave his debt, because there was no way he could pay it.

It was the same as this moment. He had broken something last night. Perhaps he had been steadily breaking it over the past five years. He wasn't sure there was any way to fix it. And so, instead he would ask for forgiveness. And offer something in return.

"Tell me," Lucy said, her voice thin.

"I hated Christmas as a child. It was so happy and warm. It was everything I was not. A display of all I could not have. It made me want. It made me feel. It made me ache. To be tantalized by all that you cannot have from your very earliest memory… There was a point where I decided I would never do that again. I would no longer want—I would have. And I would do what needed to be done to obtain the means to make it possible. Then I met you. And I… I acquired you. As I have done many things in the past."

"I'm not certain I find that flattering."

"It isn't. Simply the reasoning of a frightened man." He drew a deep breath. "We were married for five years. And I never once brought a Christmas tree or anything festive at all into our house, did I?"

"No," she said.

"It is because I didn't want to ache anymore. Reminders of the past…of that longing… They only made me ache and so I kept them away. But I couldn't stop that pain forever."

"You couldn't?"

"No. Because of you. You are my Christmas, Lucy Kennewick."

"I'm your what?"

"You are my Christmas. Being near you, so close to you, and yet not having you made me ache. So I pretended I didn't need you. I pretended you weren't important. When in truth all I really wanted was one moment of the warmth, of the happiness, I knew I could find in you." He cleared his throat. "But I was afraid. Afraid of wanting something I might not be able to have. You were right, in many ways. I am just a boy afraid of being denied."

Lucy felt as though her heart was going to explode. She stepped out the door, wrapping her arms around Nico, squeezing her eyes shut tight. "Oh, Nico. You don't have to be afraid of me. You don't have to be afraid of not having me."

"When you asked for your divorce... I told myself I hated you. Because yet again I was being denied. So I decided I wouldn't think of you. I wouldn't remember you. I wouldn't want you. Because it was better than the pain." He looked away. "Of course... I could not let go entirely. It's why I wore the ring still. Because I didn't want it to be over, no matter what I told myself."

"I hurt you? Believe me when I tell you I had no clue I possessed the power to hurt you."

He drew back slightly, his dark eyes trained on hers. "I didn't know either. Because I worked so hard to ensure that nothing did. But you...you got beneath my defenses. You were so unexpected. A virgin in business suits who wanted a marriage of convenience. Why should I ever think I would have to protect my heart from such a creature?"

She frowned. "I am not a creature."

He leaned in and kissed her lips lightly. "Of course not."

"So what do you...? I mean... How do you feel about Christmas now?" she asked, her heart thundering heavily.

"I assume by Christmas you mean you."

"That is the metaphor."

A smile curved his lips. "Aren't you going to invite me in?"

Nico had spent the whole night wandering the city feeling tortured. Feeling as though his heart had been ripped straight out of his chest and hung up on a tree in Rockefeller Center as a macabre ornament.

And then he had asked himself what the hell he was doing, wandering the city streets in the cold when he could be with his wife. When there was a woman who loved him. A woman he knew beyond a shadow of a doubt he wanted to spend the rest of his life with.

So, he had come to her.

"I would invite you in," she said, blocking the door with her petite frame. "But there are Christmas decorations in there. And I'm not sure yet how you feel about those."

"I love them," he said, the words rough, torn from him.

Her lips went slack, rounded into an O. "You do?"

"Yes."

"Why…why did you never tell Christmas? And why did you let Christmas almost divorce you? And why did you walk out of the hotel room without saying anything when Christmas confessed its true feelings?"

"Because," he said, tugging Lucy into his arms and kissing her hard. "Because I am little more than a frightened boy. I had aspirations. I wanted things. But, Lucy, that's nothing compared to risking your heart. I didn't want to let anything or anyone hurt me, ever again. I married you because you were safe. But then it turned out you weren't. So I kept you at a distance and…and then you left me. Lucy, these past six months without you have been hell."

"They have been," she said. "I mean, for me too. Without you."

"I know I don't ever want to lose you again. And I know that means investing more than I have. I know that means giving. I know that means opening up. It means risking pain."

"But healing too," she said, tears filling her eyes. "And happiness. And love. Lots of love."

He kissed her again. "I know. It's worth the risk. And now you know my secrets. If I ever close up, if I ever turn away…"

"I'll ask you why. And you do the same for me."

"I promise."

"I love you, Nico."

His heart expanded in his chest. "I love you too, Lucy. Stay my wife. Please."

"I will." She kissed him again and he looked beyond her, through the door and at the house inside. He could see a Christmas tree, lights twinkling everywhere. And he knew for a fact Christmas would never again be a promise not kept.

It would be, for him, the ultimate symbol of vows honored.

"Now maybe you should come inside," she said, a smile on her face. "I have a present for you that you might want to unwrap."

* * * * *

COMING NEXT MONTH FROM

⬧ HARLEQUIN
Presents®

Available December 15, 2015

#3393 THE QUEEN'S NEW YEAR SECRET
Princes of Petras
by Maisey Yates
The fairy tale is over for all of Petras when Queen Tabitha—
refusing to live in a loveless marriage—asks her husband for a
divorce. But anger erupts into passion, and when Tabitha flees
the palace she's carrying King Kairos's heir!

#3394 THE COST OF THE FORBIDDEN
Irresistible Russian Tycoons
by Carol Marinelli
Ruthless Sev Derzhavin is master of getting whatever—and
whomever—he wants. He's never been refused before, so
when his personal assistant Naomi resigns, Sev can't resist the
challenge of *enticing* the beautiful brunette to stay.

#3395 THESEUS DISCOVERS HIS HEIR
The Kalliakis Crown
by Michelle Smart
Stunning Joanne Brooks's arrival on Agon has given the royal
family more than they bargained for...she's the mother of
Prince Theseus's secret love child! How will she react now that
the commanding prince wants to claim his heir *and* his bride?

#3396 NEW YEAR AT THE BOSS'S BIDDING
by Rachael Thomas
Tilly Rogers is thrilled to be offered a prestigious contract for
billionaire Xavier Moretti's New Year's Eve party—until she ends
up snowbound alone with her boss! The notorious playboy
makes it his resolution to seduce virgin Tilly...

HPCNM1215RA

#3397 AWAKENING THE RAVENSDALE HEIRESS
The Ravensdale Scandals
by Melanie Milburne

Miranda Ravensdale's first love ended in tragedy, so she vowed to bury her heart with the memories. No man has broken through her facade—until billionaire Leandro Allegretti! Leandro plans to coax her dormant sensuality into life, kiss by seductive kiss...

#3398 WEARING THE DE ANGELIS RING
The Italian Titans
by Cathy Williams

Tycoon Theo De Angelis lives by his own rules...until a family debt forces him into matrimony! Beautiful, inexperienced Alexa Caldini is determined to impose ground rules on their inconvenient arrangement, but how long before Alexa's rules go up in smoke?

#3399 THE MARRIAGE HE MUST KEEP
The Wrong Heirs
by Dani Collins

Alessandro Ferrante was pleasantly surprised to discover passion in his convenient marriage to shy heiress Octavia. But when their fragile union is tested, Alessandro *must* seduce his wife again and ensure Octavia—and his child—are his forever!

#3400 MISTRESS OF HIS REVENGE
Bought by the Brazilian
by Chantelle Shaw

Cruz Delgado is the renowned owner of a diamond empire—and aristocratic Sabrina Bancroft is the *only* woman ever to have walked away from the tempting tycoon. When Cruz sees a chance, he takes his revenge...by making her his mistress!

YOU CAN FIND MORE INFORMATION ON UPCOMING HARLEQUIN® TITLES, FREE EXCERPTS AND MORE AT WWW.HARLEQUIN.COM.

HPCNM1215RB

REQUEST YOUR FREE BOOKS!

HARLEQUIN

Presents

2 FREE NOVELS PLUS
2 FREE GIFTS!

YES! Please send me 2 FREE Harlequin Presents® novels and my 2 FREE gifts (gifts are worth about $10). After receiving them, if I don't wish to receive any more books, I can return the shipping statement marked "cancel." If I don't cancel, I will receive 6 brand-new novels every month and be billed just $4.30 per book in the U.S. or $5.24 per book in Canada. That's a saving of at least 13% off the cover price! It's quite a bargain! Shipping and handling is just 50¢ per book in the U.S. and 75¢ per book in Canada.* I understand that accepting the 2 free books and gifts places me under no obligation to buy anything. I can always return a shipment and cancel at any time. Even if I never buy another book, the two free books and gifts are mine to keep forever.

106/306 HDN GHRP

Name	(PLEASE PRINT)

Address	Apt. #

City	State/Prov.	Zip/Postal Code

Signature (if under 18, a parent or guardian must sign)

Mail to the **Reader Service**:
IN U.S.A.: P.O. Box 1867, Buffalo, NY 14240-1867
IN CANADA: P.O. Box 609, Fort Erie, Ontario L2A 5X3

**Are you a current subscriber to Harlequin Presents® books
and want to receive the larger-print edition?
Call 1-800-873-8635 or visit www.ReaderService.com.**

* Terms and prices subject to change without notice. Prices do not include applicable taxes. Sales tax applicable in N.Y. Canadian residents will be charged applicable taxes. Offer not valid in Quebec. This offer is limited to one order per household. Not valid for current subscribers to Harlequin Presents books. All orders subject to credit approval. Credit or debit balances in a customer's account(s) may be offset by any other outstanding balance owed by or to the customer. Please allow 4 to 6 weeks for delivery. Offer available while quantities last.

Your Privacy—The Reader Service is committed to protecting your privacy. Our Privacy Policy is available online at www.ReaderService.com or upon request from the Reader Service.

We make a portion of our mailing list available to reputable third parties that offer products we believe may interest you. If you prefer that we not exchange your name with third parties, or if you wish to clarify or modify your communication preferences, please visit us at www.ReaderService.com/consumerschoice or write to us at Reader Service Preference Service, P.O. Box 9062, Buffalo, NY 14240-9062. Include your complete name and address.

SPECIAL EXCERPT FROM

✦HARLEQUIN

Presents®

Can King Kairos claim his heir and convince his beautiful queen Tabitha that they're bound by duty, passion and love, before the clock strikes midnight on their fairy tale?

Read on for a sneak preview of
THE QUEEN'S NEW YEAR SECRET,
the final book in **Maisey Yates**'s *sensational duet*
PRINCES OF PETRAS.

"I don't think we've ever…really been alone before."

"We are very often alone," he said, frowning.

"In a palace filled with hundreds, in a building other people live in."

"I have never kidnapped you before, either. You've also never been pregnant with my baby. Oh, yes, and we have never been on the brink of divorce. So, a season of firsts. How nice to add this to the list."

She stood up, stretching out her stiff muscles. "Where exactly do you get off being angry at me? We are here because of you."

"I'm angry with you because this divorce is happening at your demand."

"Had I not demanded we divorce, I wouldn't be pregnant."

"Had you not frozen me out of your bed, perhaps you would have been pregnant a couple of months sooner."

She gritted her teeth, reckless heat pouring through her veins. "How dare you?" She advanced on him, and he wrapped his arm around her waist, pulling her close. "Don't."

Her protest was cut off by the press of his mouth against hers, hot and uncompromising, his tongue staking a claim as he took her deep, hard. She had no idea where these kinds of kisses had come from. Who this man was. This man who would spirit her away to a private island. Who kissed her like he was a dying man and her lips held his salvation.

He kissed her neck, down to her collarbone, retracing that same path with the tip of his tongue. She found herself tearing at his shirt, her heart thundering hard, every fiber of her being desperate to have him. Desperate to have him inside her again. Like that night in his office. That night when the promise that had been broken on their wedding night was finally fulfilled.

Don't miss
THE QUEEN'S NEW YEAR SECRET by Maisey Yates,
available January 2016 wherever
Harlequin Presents® books and ebooks are sold.

www.Harlequin.com

HARLEQUIN Presents®

Kidnapped by her king!

The fairy tale is over for all of Petras when Queen Tabitha— refusing to live in a loveless marriage—asks her husband for a divorce. But anger erupts into passion, and when Tabitha flees the palace she's carrying King Kairos's heir!

SAVE $1.00

on the purchase of THE QUEEN'S NEW YEAR SECRET by Maisey Yates {available Dec. 15, 2015} or any other Harlequin Presents® book.

Redeemable at participating outlets in the U.S. and Canada only. Not redeemable at Barnes & Noble stores. Limit one coupon per customer.

52613177

5 65373 00076 2 (8100)0 12108

COUPON EXPIRES JAN. 4, 2016

Available wherever books are sold, including most bookstores, supermarkets, drugstores and discount stores.

www.Harlequin.com

HARLEQUIN

Presents®

Don't miss Rachael Thomas's thrilling new temptation-filled story, as a snowbound New Year's Eve explodes into a night of forbidden passion with the boss!

Jilted bride Tilly Rogers is thrilled to be offered a prestigious catering contract for billionaire Xavier Moretti's New Year's Eve party…until she ends up snowbound and at her boss's bidding!

It's the end of the year *and* the end of Tilly's contract—leaving Xavier free to seduce her! Hardly shy of a challenge, this notorious playboy makes it his resolution to have virgin Tilly crumbling under his experienced touch.

Find out what happens next in

NEW YEAR AT THE BOSS'S BIDDING

January 2016

Stay Connected:

Harlequin.com

iHeartPresents.com

🇫 /HarlequinBooks

🐦 @HarlequinBooks

📌 /HarlequinBooks

HP13402